BEST BOOKS 倍斯特出版事業有限公司 Best Publishing Ltd.

雅思單字聖經

模擬試題

Amanda Chou ◎ 著

英式發音 QRCODE
DOWNLOAD

獨創 **單字複選題** 和聽、讀整合試題
確實理解、秒對應到關鍵考點，考取 **9.0高分**

藉由單字複選題，達到閱讀100%理解

規劃**單字複選題**，在無法仰賴刪除法或猜對的情況下演練試題，提升**靈活思考力**，遇到各種變化題均能「**巧妙**」應對。

段落填空和聽讀整合強化，優化大腦處理資訊能力

收錄更具**鑑別度的試題**，融合**聽、讀關鍵**，遇到單純僅有閱讀或聽力的試題都能得心應手。

PRE FACE 作者序

　　本書以三個面向強化考生的字彙能力，有別於單字搭配例句的學習性單字書籍。當中包含了❶同義字模擬試題、❷填空題模擬試題以及❸聽、讀整合能力強化。同義字模擬試題適用於各種程度的考生，以最基礎的練習方式，協助考生閱讀例句並且理解，在「試題中畫底線的字彙」和「選項中的字彙」做連結，藉由背誦同反義字彙後，迅速具備在幾秒內答對試題的能力。這類的試題雖然也常見於轉學考等考試中，但是要確實提升程度跟鑑別出考生能力，在較有難度的考試中，則會刪除這類試題。尤其是在雅思和新托福試題中，具備這樣的能力只是基礎，因為這類試題僅能算是最基礎的同義轉換練習。像在雅思閱讀和聽力測驗中，不太會有這樣直接對應的考題，也就是送分題給考生。試題則包含了各種程度的同義轉換，有些甚至非常隱晦難答，用以區別考生能力是在 7.5-8.0 還是 8.0-8.5。

　　要如何進一步提升呢?不是光靠背誦很多字彙或是具備基礎同義轉換就能答對。關於這部分，就需要具備更進階的單字訓練，也就是這本書規劃的❷填空題模擬試題或是另一本《雅思單字聖經》第一部分的雙填空試題，這兩部份的差異點在於「雙填空試題」可以用於提升雅思和 SAT 閱讀答題。寫作能力和語法好的考生，仍可以使用文法等技巧以及刪除法答對試題。本書的「填空題模擬試題」則是複選題，在同個題目中，確實可能有兩個正確的單字答案，所以考生必須確實理解才能答對試題，考生或許在部分試題上可以用刪除法，但還是需要本身的語文能力來解題。藉由這兩種試題的規劃，考生就能理解為什麼自己在寫完官方試題對答案，考試分數未能提升的真正原因，因為還是需要仰賴好幾個階段的字彙和閱讀訓練後，考生才確實具備能在下次閱讀考試時考取更高的成績，而非報考數次雅思閱讀成績仍停留在 7.0 分而大惑不解。

　　關於「**聽、讀整合能力強化**」則與《雅思單字聖經》的規劃相同，但主題不同，所想要更多練習的考生可以兩本一起閱讀。這部分源於聽和讀的能力是有相關聯。單一仰賴寫聽力試題或是僅撰寫閱讀試題，在學習上是事倍功半的。因為大腦僅使用了單一訓練規劃，而「**聽、讀整合能力強化**」則涵蓋聽和讀必須並用，寫同分試題就包含這兩個規劃。考生務必要聽試題後，撰寫答案，並於寫完聽力後接續演練閱讀，檢視在同篇文章中，聽和讀的答題落差。考生只要大量持之以恆以這種方式進行訓練，就能迅速打通聽和讀的學習關鍵，逐步理解出這兩個能力的關聯性。相信在藉由書中的演練後，考生就能迅速脫胎換骨，寫官方試題時，有不一樣的感受，更能抓住考點，與僅拿著官方試題猛寫，但每次撰寫僅浪費一次真題且沒有確實提升理解能力的考生有所區隔。因為每寫一次官方試題，加上檢討錯誤，考生一定會記住部分脈絡，這樣就會失去準度，也就是你寫過的官方試題回數就不能再當成能正確檢視你本身程度的考題了。所以還是蠻建議考生先演練這本和其他公司的相關雅思書籍，提升了聽力和閱讀理解力後，在訂好每天撰寫官方試題的排程進行密集的演練，最後獲取佳績。

Amanda Chou

真題重現
精選雅思「聽＋讀」循環出現單字
且有中英對照
各階段學習者均適用，迅速累積上百同義字彙

· 規劃符合各階段學習者需求的字彙測驗，並融入上百個雅思真題字彙，並錄音，在備考更為無往不利，聽＋讀狂飆平均八以上成績，反覆聽誦更能快速累積語感和寫作實力。

超狂獨創複選題考題
強化考生綜合答題實力和確實理解力
鑑別各程度考生
穩操勝卷地應對各類型英語測驗

· 具鑑別度的考題才能檢視是否確實理解，而非僅仰賴答題技巧和運氣答對題目，有效提升考生在實際考生的臨場反應和答題實力，一次就搞定雅思測驗。

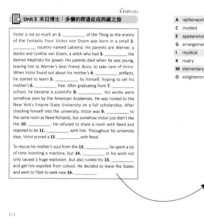

🎧 MP3 031

📖 Unit 3 末日博士：多變的際遇促成西藏之旅

Victor is not so much an **1.** _____ of the Thing as the enemy of the Fantastic Four. Victor von Doom was born in a small **2.** _____ country named Latveria. His parents are Werner, a doctor and Cynthia von Doom, a witch who had **3.** _____ the demon Mephisto for power. His parents died when he was young, leaving him to Werner's best friend, Boris, to take care of Victor. When Victor found out about his mother's **4.** _____ artifacts, he started to learn **5.** _____ by himself, hoping to set his mother's **6.** _____ free. After graduating from **7.** _____ school, he became a scientific **8.** _____. His works were somehow seen by the American Academies. He was invited to the New York's Empire State University on a full scholarship. After checking himself into the university, Victor was **9.** _____ to the same room as Reed Richards, but somehow Victor just didn't like the **10.** _____. He refused to share a room with Reed and rejected to be **11.** _____ with him. Throughout his university days, Victor pursued a **12.** _____ with Reed.

To rescue his mother's soul from the **13.** _____, he spent a lot of time inventing a machine, but **14.** _____ in his work not only caused a huge explosion, but also ruined his **15.** _____ and get him expelled from school. He decided to leave the States and went to Tibet to seek new **16.** _____.

214

A	netherworld	B	genius
C	invoked	D	soul
E	appearance	F	enemy
G	arrangement	H	assigned
I	mystical	J	sorcery
K	rivalry	L	friends
M	elementary	N	European
O	enlightenment	P	miscalculation

Unit 3 末日博士：多變的際遇促成西藏之旅

Part 1 同義字檢視試題

Part 2 填空題檢測試

海量試題
「聽＋讀」雙重整合能力強化
同一試題雙軌提升兩個單項成績

· 獨家規劃試題，將聽＋讀的關聯性大幅強化，持續練習能強化大腦，同步提升對於兩個單項的整合答題實力，確實將書中的練習徹底運用後再寫官方試題，能發揮更大效果，並提升信心。

▶ 中譯：

富有農場主人約翰和伊麗莎白·豪利特的兒子，詹姆斯·豪利特出生在加拿大阿爾伯塔省的冷湖。詹姆斯確巧看到場地管理人，湯瑪斯·洛根毆害約翰·豪利，這是第一次，詹姆斯的爪子從他的手背延伸，他真常兇猛的攻擊入侵者，他殺死了湯瑪斯，洛根，並在湯格的臉上留下三個爪痕。詹姆斯後來就採用了「洛根」這個名字，以隱藏自己的身份。洛根和他的童年玩伴羅絲最終墜入愛河。然而，在湯瑪斯·洛根的兒子道根前來對戰時，意外發生了，他的爪子偶然地殺害了羅絲，他只好離開羅絲，生活在真正荒野的狼群中。洛根是一個突變體，他有著相當名的狼爪，擁有動物敏銳的感覺，進階的體能，和稱為癒合因子強大的再生能力。

爾後，他在軍隊裡被植入了假的記憶體。直到他加入加拿大大國防部才掙脫了精神控制。然而，他開始作為一個情報人員並和加拿大政府合作，成為加拿大的第一位超級英雄，金剛狼。

256

Unit 13 金鋼狼：猛爪的發現、再生能力

▶ 參考答案

1.	F	2.	L
3.	D	4.	H
5.	A	6.	B
7.	G	8.	J
9.	C	10.	P
11.	K	12.	E
13.	I		
15.	N		

Part 1 同義字檢視試題

Part

閱讀附中譯
便於考生學習，亦可用於中英互譯練習
提升翻譯寫作實力
打通讀＋寫任督二脈

· 除了聽讀雙軌測驗外，閱讀附有中譯，有效運用在寫作和翻譯上，能快速強化雅思寫作能力。閱讀也附錄音，反覆聆聽可以快速提升語感，同步強化雅思閱讀答題實力。

目次 CONTENTS

1 Part 同義字模擬試題

2 Part
填空題模擬試題

3 Part
聽、讀整合能力強化

UNIT 1 模擬試題（一）

✎ Vocabulary in Context

MP3 001

1. The newly elected administration has launched an aggressive _____ for federal counterterrorism in hopes of solidifying national security.
   Planning is in the closest meaning to this word.
   A. transaction   C. strategy
   B. prejudice   D. disconnection

2. The research findings about hypnosis healing remain inconclusive and _____; therefore, the curing method still has a long way to go.
   Debatable is in the closest meaning to this word.
   A. potential   C. magnificent
   B. anxious   D. controversial

3. Animal rights groups _____ to take more drastic measures unless the cosmetic manufactures stopped inhumane animal tests.
   Announced is in the closest meaning to this word.
   A. claimed   C. surrendered
   B. unraveled   D. liberated

4. The Internet's _____ among adolescents brought about serious academic and personality problems and has gradually aroused social attention.
   Dependence is in the closest meaning to this word.

A. governance
B. addiction
C. retreat
D. provocation

1. 新上任的內閣已經推動積極的國家反恐策略，為的是希望鞏固國家安全。

Planning 的意思最接近於這個字。

A. 交易　　　　　C. **策略**
B. 偏見　　　　　D. 中斷

2. 有關於催眠治療的研究發現依舊是未定且有爭議的；因此，這種治療方式仍有待努力。

Debatable 的意思最接近於這個字。

A. 有潛力的　　　C. 壯麗的
B. 焦慮的　　　　D. **有爭議的**

3. 動物權益團體宣稱，除非化妝品製造廠商停止不人道的動物實驗，否則將採取更激烈的手段，。

Announced 的意思最接近於這個字。

A. **宣稱**　　　　C. 投降
B. 闡明　　　　　D. 解放

4. 青少年的網路成癮導致嚴重的課業及人格問題，並且逐漸地引發社會關切。

Dependence 的意思最接近於這個字。

A. 管理　　　　　C. 撤退
B. **上癮**　　　　D. 挑釁

答案　**1.** C　**2.** D　**3.** A　**4.** B

Part 1 同義字模擬試題

Part 2 填空題模擬試題

Part 3 聽、讀整合能力強化

5. Thanks to the decreased costs of 3D printers, the technology of the three-dimensional printing has recently gained _____ among different fields of industry.
Prevalence is in the closest meaning to this word.
A. richness   C. manipulation
B. popularity   D. capability

6. The financial institution posted an advertisement to offer jobs for business school graduates with _____ consciousness and abilities.
Creative is in the closest meaning to this word.
A. rigid   C. optional
B. innovative   D. retrospective

7. Young generations should be taught from their early childhood to practice the 3R _____ — Reduce, Reuse, and Recycle to protect and sustain the earth.
Regulations is in the closest meaning to this word.
A. Groups   C. Principles
B. Facilities   D. Restrictions

8. Mr. Banks is a lawyer _____ in criminal laws and is dedicated to defending against criminal charges.
Professionalized is in the closest meaning to this word.
A. franchised   C. abolished
B. managed   D. specialized

5. 幸虧有 3D 立體印刷機的降價，3D 立體印刷科技近日在各個不同產業領域受到歡迎。

Prevalence 的意思最接近於這個字。

A. 財富　　　　　C. 操弄

B. 受歡迎　　　D. 能力

6. 這家經融機構刊登職缺廣告來徵求具創新意識及能力的商學院畢業生。

Creative 的意思最接近於這個字。

A. 僵化的　　　　C. 可選擇的

B. 創新的　　　D. 回顧的

7. 年輕世代應從小被教導力行 3R 原則 — 減量、重複使用，以及回收，以保護並延續地球。

Regulations 的意思最接近於這個字。

A. 團體　　　　　**C. 原則**

B. 設施　　　　　D. 限制

8. 班克斯先生是一名專精於刑事訴訟法的律師，並致力於刑事訴訟的辯護。

Professionalized 的意思最接近於這個字。

A. 加盟　　　　　C. 廢除

B. 設法　　　　　**D. 專攻**

答案　**5.** B　**6.** B　**7.** C　**8.** D

9. The dazzling northern lights, also called "the aurora borealis," display as one of nature's greatest spectacles, and are _____ to only certain regions in Canada, Scotland, Norway, and Sweden.
Special is in the closest meaning to this word.
A. unique   C. practical
B. conceptual   D. invisible

10. After surviving the horrible plane crash, Pamela came to realize the value of life and was _____ to social charity causes.
Changed is in the closest meaning to this word.
A. emigrated   C. improved
B. navigated   D. converted

11. The refined merchandise exhibited in the Trade Fair last month was _____ by Morrison Company and has received great numbers of orders since then.
Produced is in the closest meaning to this word.
A. approached   C. manufactured
B. combined   D. rejected

12. The rich and renowned CEO remained modest and was _____ about charitable affairs by donating millions of dollars each year.
Zealous is in the closest meaning to this word.
A. violent   C. popular
B. indifferent   D. enthusiastic

9. 炫目的極北之光，又稱為「北極光」，展現大自然絕佳的奇觀之一，並且是加拿大、蘇格蘭、挪威及瑞典特定地區獨具的景觀。
   Special 的意思最接近於這個字。
   A. **獨特的**　　　C. 實際的
   B. 概念的　　　　D. 隱形的

10. 潘蜜拉在可怕的墜機事件倖存後，領悟到生命的可貴，並轉而致力於社會慈善工作。
    Changed 的意思最接近於這個字。
    A. 移民　　　　C. 改善
    B. 航行　　　　D. **轉變**

11. 上個月在貿易展展示的優質商品是由莫里森公司所製造的，並從那時起接獲大量的訂單。
    Produced 的意思最接近於這個字。
    A. 接近　　　　C. **製造**
    B. 結合　　　　D. 排斥

12. 這位富有且著名的執行長依舊保持謙遜的態度，並且熱心於每年捐贈數百萬元贊助慈善事業。.
    Zealous 的意思最接近於這個字。
    A. 暴力的　　　C. 受歡迎的
    B. 冷淡的　　　D. **熱忱的**

答案 **9.** A　**10.** D　**11.** C　**12.** D

模擬試題（二）

✏ Vocabulary in Context

MP3 002

13. It is _____ that producing books in hard copy format may bring several million tons of harmful CO2 into the atmosphere, so E-books are definitely here to stay.
Calculated is in the closest meaning to this word.
A. rebelled　　　　C. undertaken
B. estimated　　　　D. humiliated

14. According to neuroscientists, _____ 20 percent of short-term memory can be improved by regular physical exercise, especially to the elderly.
Roughly is in the closest meaning to this word.
A. recently　　　　C. perpetually
B. approximately　　D. ironically

15. With _____ pop music superstars creating extraordinary performances, Korean pop music trend has prevailed worldwide.
Talented is in the closest meaning to this word.
A. mandatory　　　　C. renewable
B. economical　　　　D. versatile

16. Music, with its functions of offering soothing feelings and full relaxation, remains a _____ language for all times.
General is in the closest meaning to this word.
A. separate　　　　C. defiant
B. constructive　　　D. universal

13. 據估計，製造硬皮書籍可能將數百萬公噸有害的二氧化碳氣體帶入大氣層，所以電子書當然應該普遍推廣。

Calculated 的意思最接近於這個字。

A. 反叛   C. 從事

B. 估計   D. 羞辱

14. 根據神經科學家的說法，將近百分之二十短暫的記憶可以經由規律的體能運動得到改善，尤其是對老年人而言。

Roughly 的意思最接近於這個字。

A. 近來   C. 永久地

B. 將近   D. 諷刺地

15. 有著多才多藝流行音樂超級巨星創造傑出的表演，韓國流行音樂的潮流遍及全世界。

Talented 的意思最接近於這個字。

A. 命令的   C. 可更新的

B. 節約的   **D. 多才多藝的**

16. 音樂，具有提供舒緩情緒及全面放鬆的功用，一直以來是一個世界性的語言。

General 的意思最接近於這個字。

A. 分隔的   C. 違抗的

B. 積極的   **D. 全世界的**

答案   **13.** B   **14.** B   **15.** D   **16.** D

17. Some extreme-sports enthusiasts are capable of achieving difficult and challenging extreme tasks with _____ perfection.
Unbelievable is in the closest meaning to this word.
A. synthetic
C. incredible
B. luxurious
D. thorny

18. Due to wide _____ of public opinion, the political figure caught in a dilemma had a hard time getting away from the scandal.
Changes is in the closest meaning to this word.
A. variations
C. approaches
B. solitude
D. isolation

19. The company has recently renewed the computer software, and is working on tests to make sure the new system will be _____ with the existing apparatus.
Agreeable is in the closest meaning to this word.
A. sympathetic
C. compatible
B. experimental
D. interruptible

20. Martin has lived in comfort and luxury ever since he made successful _____ investments and piled up a considerable fortune.
Pecuniary is in the closest meaning to this word.
A. financial
C. superstitious
B. profound
D. awkward

17. 有些極限運動的愛好者有能力以令人難以置信的完美方式達成艱困且具挑戰性的極限任務。

Unbelievable 的意思最接近於這個字。

A. 綜合的　　　　C. **令人難以置信的**

B. 奢華的　　　　D. 棘手的

18. 由於輿論的眾說紛紜，這位深陷進退兩難困境的政治人物很難從醜聞中脫身。

Changes 的意思最接近於這個字。

A. **變化**　　　　C. 方法

B. 孤獨　　　　　D. 隔離

19. 這家公司最近更新了電腦軟體，並正在測試以確保新的系統與現有的裝置相容。

Agreeable 的意思最接近於這個字。

A. 同情的　　　　C. **相容的**

B. 實驗的　　　　D. 可中斷的

20. 馬汀自從金融投資成功且積聚可觀的財富後，一直過著舒適奢華的生活。

Pecuniary 的意思最接近於這個字。

A. **金融的**　　　　C. 迷信的

B. 深奧的　　　　D. 笨拙的

答案 **17.** C　　**18.** A　　**19.** C　　**20.** A

21. Most volunteers are delighted to help needy people, for they can not only learn useful skills to prepare them for work but mainly _____ great pleasure from doing it.
Obtain is in the closest meaning to this word.
A. justify   C. multiply
B. abandon   D. derive

22. It's predictable that the confrontation will persistently go on since the management and the _____ failed to reach any satisfactory agreement.
Workers is in the closest meaning to this word.
A. executives   C. employees
B. individuals   D. retailers

23. Mrs. Newman planned to move to the countryside, following her doctor's advice that the rural environment might be conducive to the _____ of her health.
Recovery is in the closest meaning to this word.
A. stimulation   C. restoration
B. contribution   D. introduction

24. Given that dust storms have been _____ in huge amounts with greater forces, scientists all over the world are working on the causes and the solutions.
Created is in the closest meaning to this word.
A. accompanied   C. summoned
B. produced   D. degenerated

21. 大多數的志工樂於幫助貧困的人，目的不僅在於學習職場技能，主要是能從中得到極大的樂趣。

Obtain 的意思最接近於這個字。

A. 辯護　　　　　　C. 成倍增加

B. 拋棄　　　　　　**D. 獲得**

22. 由於管理階層和員工無法達成任何滿意的共識，雙方將會持續地抗爭是可預期的。

Workers 的意思最接近於這個字。

A. 主管　　　　　　**C. 員工**

B. 個人　　　　　　D. 零售商

23. 遵循醫生所提出關於鄉村環境有助於恢復健康的勸告，紐曼太太計畫搬到鄉下去居住。

Recovery 的意思最接近於這個字。

A. 刺激　　　　　　**C. 復原**

B. 貢獻　　　　　　D. 介紹

24. 考慮到沙塵暴以更強的威力大量地成形中，世界各地的科學家正努力於探討成因及解決之道。

Created 的意思最接近於這個字。

A. 陪伴　　　　　　C. 召喚

B. 生產　　　　　D. 衰退

答案　**21.** D　**22.** C　**23.** C　**24.** B

3 UNIT

模擬試題（三）

✎ Vocabulary in Context

MP3 003

25. During the process of brainstorming, several _____ solutions to the thorny problem were eventually worked out.
Useful is in the closest meaning to this word.
A. practical   C. superficial
B. rectangular   D. competitive

26. The sudden collapse of the bridge during the rush hour was the major cause of the severe _____ to the commuters and passers-by.
Damage is in the closest meaning to this word.
A. continuity   C. magnitude
B. illnesses   D. injuries

27. Cathy had a hard time writing her thesis, for her professor requested that she should _____ her argument with more exact and innovative points of view.
Strengthen is in the closest meaning to this word.
A. reinforce   C. meditate
B. correspond   D. familiarize

28. Luke _____ on the idea that people should protect rare and extinct animals, and he constantly sponsored campaigns of the kind.

Held is in the closest meaning to this word.

A. commenced

C. negotiated

B. fastened

D. ridiculed

25. 腦力激盪的過程中，數種解決這個棘手問題的實用方案終於被激盪出來。

Useful 的意思最接近於這個字。

A. **實用的**

C. 膚淺的

B. 矩形的

D. 競爭的

26. 在交通尖峰期間，橋梁突然的倒塌是造成通勤族和行人嚴重傷害的主因。

Damage 的意思最接近於這個字。

A. 持續

C. 強度

B. 疾病

D. **傷害**

27. 凱西寫論文寫得很辛苦，因為她的教授要求她應該使用更確切且更創新的觀點來加強論證。

Strengthen 的意思最接近於這個字。

A. **加強**

C. 沉思

B. 通信

D. 熟悉

28. 路克堅持於人們應該保護稀有瀕臨絕種動物的想法，並且時常贊助此種類型的活動。

Held 的意思最接近於這個字。

A. 開始

C. 協商

B. **堅持**

D. 挪揄

答案 25. A　26. D　27. A　28. B

29. The private art gallery, seemingly a building of small scale, had a(n) _____ large collection of Oriental and Western paintings.
Surprisingly is in the closest meaning to this word.
A. eventually   C. inevitably
B. amazingly   D. automatically

30. The company aimed at recruiting new staff members familiar with international trade and fluent with Japanese, since the Japanese market _____ for 40% of its revenue.
Occupied is in the closest meaning to this word.
A. prescribed   C. accounted
B. explored   D. restrained

31. It's amazing that nowadays consumers can _____ almost anything through shopping websites on the Internet.
Buy is in the closest meaning to this word.
A. purchase   C. rehearse
B. adopt   D. coordinate

32. Electronic products _____ from Japan have always received great welcome because they tend to be functional and durable.
Introduced is in the closest meaning to this word.
A. imported   C. appreciated
B. settled   D. vaccinated

29. 這間私人經營的藝術畫廊，表面上似乎是座小規模的建築，卻有著驚人數量東西方畫作的收藏。
Surprisingly 的意思最接近於這個字。
A. 最終地
B. **驚人地**
C. 無可避免地
D. 自動地

30. 由於日本市場佔了公司收入的百分之四十，這家公司的目標是招募熟悉國際貿易以及精通日語的新職員。
*Occupied*的意思最接近於這個字。
A. 開藥方
B. 探索
C. **佔...**
D. 限制

31. 今日而言，消費者能夠透過網際網路的購物網站購買得到幾乎任何東西是很驚人的。
Buy 的意思最接近於這個字。
A. **購買**
B. 採用
C. 預演
D. 協調

32. 從日本進口的電子產品一向大受歡迎，因為他們的產品既實用又耐用。
Introduced 的意思最接近於這個字。
A. **進口**
B. 定居
C. 欣賞
D. 接種疫苗

答案 **29.** B　**30.** C　**31.** A　**32.** A

33. The Anderson family decided to _____ to Australia to try their luck and start a new life there.
Move is in the closest meaning to this word.
A. suspend   C. reconcile
B. qualify   D. emigrate

34. Kevin's doctor warned him of the fact that improper diet and living habits may pose _____ danger to his health.
Possible is in the closest meaning to this word.
A. appropriate   C. potential
B. discriminated   D. trustworthy

35. With the violent hurricane _____, residents were advised to take immediate precautions.
Advancing is in the closest meaning to this word.
A. vanishing   C. approaching
B. contrasting   D. renovating

36. The _____ of technology to our daily life enables us to live comfortably and joyfully.
Utilization is in the closest meaning to this word.
A. glamour   C. monotony
B. sophistication   D. application

33. 安德森一家人決定移民到澳洲去謀求發展並試圖在那裡展開新生活。

Move 的意思最接近於這個字。

A. 懸掛　　　　　　C. 妥協

B. 合格　　　　　　**D. 移民**

34. 凱文的醫生警告他不適當的飲食以及生活習慣可能對他的健康造成潛在的危險。

Possible 的意思最接近於這個字。

A. 適當的　　　　　**C. 潛在的**

B. 歧視的　　　　　D. 值得信賴的

35. 隨著猛烈颶風的逼近，居民被建議採取立即的預防措施。

Advancing 的意思最接近於這個字。

A. 消失　　　　　　**C. 接近**

B. 對照　　　　　　D. 整修

36. 把科技運用於我們的日常生活中促使我們能夠過著舒適及享受的生活。

Utilization 的意思最接近於這個字。

A. 魅力　　　　　　C. 單調

B. 世故　　　　　　**D. 應用**

答案　**33.** D　**34.** C　**35.** C　**36.** D

模擬試題（四）

✏ Vocabulary in Context

37. Irene had better watch out for those her gossip friends who may once in a while _____ rumors about her.
Scatter is in the closest meaning to this word.
A. decorate   C. pacify
B. spread   D. experience

38. At the present time, scientists spare no efforts to find resources of the alternative energy to substitute for the fossil fuels _____ by industry.
Exhausted is in the closest meaning to this word.
A. occurred   C. represented
B. consumed   D. prospered

39. After most of its safety _____ failed to meet the standards, the mall was seriously penalized and had to make immediate improvement.
Examination is in the closest meaning to this word.
A. motivation   C. purification
B. inspections   D. concessions

40. Compared with others, people tortured by depression _____ need more care and attention, for they don't easily reveal their emotional problems.
Comparatively is in the closest meaning to this word.
A. viciously   C. relatively
B. competently   D. punctually

37. 艾琳最好要小心她那群偶爾會散播有關於她謠言的八卦朋友。

Scatter 的意思最接近於這個字。

A. 裝飾　　　　　C. 平和

B. 散播　　　　D. 經歷

38. 目前來說，科學家們不遺餘力地尋找替代能源的資源來取代工業所消耗的化石燃料。

Exhausted 的意思最接近於這個字。

A. 發生　　　　　C. 代表

B. 消耗　　　　D. 繁榮

39. 在大部分的安全檢驗無法符合標準之後，這個大賣場被嚴厲地處罰，並且必須做立即的改善。

Examination 的意思最接近於這個字。

A. 動機　　　　　C. 淨化

B. 檢查　　　　D. 讓步

40. 和一般人比較起來，為憂鬱症所苦的人相對地需要更多的關心和注意，因為他們不輕易地透露他們的情緒問題。

Comparatively 的意思最接近於這個字。

A. 邪惡地　　　　**C. 相對地**

B. 勝任地　　　　D. 準時地

答案　**37.** B　**38.** B　**39.** B　**40.** C

Part 1 同義字模擬試題

Part 2 填空題模擬試題

Part 3 聽、讀整合能力強化

41. To keep healthy, one should be careful not to consume too much the food that _____ additives, such as preservatives, coloring, or artificial flavorings.
Includes is in the closest meaning to this word.
A. contains   C. huddles
B. digests   D. transforms

42. The manager informed the factory that they might _____ or even cancel the original orders if the goods shipped in continued to be in poor quality.
Reduce is in the closest meaning to this word.
A. resolve   C. withhold
B. approve   D. decrease

43. To make both ends meet, Roy had no choice but to take several part-time jobs to _____ additional income.
Produce is in the closest meaning to this word.
A. despise   C. generate
B. supervise   D. overlook

44. The magician's _____ performances attracted full attention of the audience and won him long and loud applause.
Wonderful is in the closest meaning to this word.
A. marvelous   C. reckless
B. exclusive   D. feasible

41. 為了維持健康，人們應該小心不要吃太多含有添加物的食物，例如：防腐劑、色素，或者人工調味料。

Includes 的意思最接近於這個字。

A. **包含**　　　　C. 蜷縮
B. 消化　　　　　D. 轉變

42. 經理通知工廠，假使進貨的商品仍舊品質不良的話，他們會減少或甚至取消原有的訂單。

Reduce 的意思最接近於這個字。

A. 下定決心　　　C. 阻擋
B. 贊同　　　　　D. **減少**

43. 為了收支均衡，羅伊不得不兼職數份兼差的工作來賺取額外的收入。

Produce 的意思最接近於這個字。

A. 鄙視　　　　　C. **產生**
B. 監督　　　　　D. 忽略

44. 魔術師奇妙的表演吸引全場觀眾的目光，並且為自己贏得許久響亮的喝采聲。

Wonderful 的意思最接近於這個字。

A. **奇妙的**　　　C. 粗率的
B. 獨家的　　　　D. 可行的

答案 **41.** A　**42.** D　**43.** C　**44.** A

45. People who _____ from a migraine can relieve the pain effectively by all forms of relaxation, a lot of water-drinking, or keeping away from noises and bright lights.
Torture is in the closest meaning to this word.
A. guarantee   C. proceed
B. suffer   D. investigate

46. Mr. Cosby had a serious cold and coughed a lot; thus, he could hardly _____ anything because of the painful throat.
Gulp is in the closest meaning to this word.
A. fumble   C. swallow
B. console   D. nominate

47. The movie adapted from a novel was disappointing to the moviegoers because they could hardly find any _____ between the two.
Correspondence is in the closest meaning to this word.
A. insistence   C. integrity
B. metabolism   D. consistency

48. In my opinion, to settle the dispute, all you need to do is come out and clarify your stand on the controversial _____.
Problem is in the closest meaning to this word.
A. vacancy   C. revision
B. issue   D. diagnosis

45. 罹患偏頭痛的人可以藉由各種放鬆的方式，喝大量的水，或遠離噪音及亮光來有效地紓緩疼痛。

Torture 的意思最接近於這個字。

A. 保證　　　　　C. 行進

B. **受苦**　　　　　D. 調查

46. 寇斯比先生由於嚴重的感冒加上咳嗽咳得厲害，以致於喉嚨疼痛而無法吞嚥任何東西。

Gulp 的意思最接近於這個字。

A. 摸索　　　　　C. **吞嚥**

B. 安慰　　　　　D. 提名

47. 這部由小說改編的電影讓電影觀賞者感到失望，因為他們幾乎找不出兩者間情節相符之處。

Correspondence 的意思最接近於這個字。

A. 堅持　　　　　C. 廉潔

B. 新陳代謝　　　D. **一致性**

48. 依我之見，為了解決紛爭，你所必須做的是出面並澄清你對於這個具有爭議性議題的立場。

Problem 的意思最接近於這個字。

A. 空缺　　　　　C. 修訂

B. **議題**　　　　　D. 診斷

答案　**45.** B　**46.** C　**47.** D　**48.** B

模擬試題（五）

UNIT 5

Vocabulary in Context

MP3 005

49. After a long separation from each other since senior high, Julie had a surprising and pleasant _____ with Alex.
   Meeting is in the closest meaning to this word.
   A. machinery   C. reputation
   B. encounter   D. assortment

50. It is imperative that we humans put emphasis on ecological _____ and set up as many wildlife reserves as we can.
   Protection is in the closest meaning to this word.
   A. authority   C. tranquility
   B. frustration   D. preservation

51. As an optimistic and diligent college graduate, James is willing to explore a new working field and take up _____ tasks.
   Confronting is in the closest meaning to this word.
   A. challenging   C. prompt
   B. stubborn   D. easy-going

52. The world surrounding us is a seriously _____ one, and we must take precautions to cope with the global ecological crisis.
   Polluted is in the closest meaning to this word.
   A. released   C. contaminated
   B. outdated   D. engaged

49. 自從高中彼此分開一段長時間後，茱莉和艾力克斯有一次驚喜且愉快的邂逅。

Meeting 的意思最接近於這個字。

A. 機械　　　　　C. 名譽

B. **偶遇**　　　　　D. 分類

50. 我們人類現在急需要做的是重視生態保育並且盡可能多設置野生動物保護區。

Protection 的意思最接近於這個字。

A. 權威　　　　　C. 寧靜

B. 挫折　　　　　D. **保存**

51. 身為一名樂觀且勤奮的大學畢業生，詹姆斯很樂意去探索新的工作領域並承擔具挑戰性的任務。

Confronting 的意思最接近於這個字。

A. **挑戰的**　　　C. 快速的

B. 固執的　　　　D. 隨和的

52. 環繞在我們周遭的是一個嚴重污染的世界，我們必須採取預防措施來對抗全球的生態危機。

Polluted 的意思最接近於這個字。

A. 釋放的　　　　C. **汙染的**

B. 過時的　　　　D. 忙於…的

答案 **49.** B　　**50.** D　　**51.** A　　**52.** C

53. Scientists are _____ robots with multiple functions to provide services that can meet varied needs of all the users.

Producing is in the closest meaning to this word.

A. developing   C. hallmarking

B. objecting   D. perishing

54. The applicant's additional language skills and working experience definitely _____ the chance of being employed.

Add is in the closest meaning to this word.

A. abbreviate   C. occupy

B. increase   D. withstand

55. To _____ the risk of clogged arteries and heart attacks, one had better get away from trans fats, which may cause the rise of cholesterol in the blood.

Decrease is in the closest meaning to this word.

A. reduce   C. conclude

B. accumulate   D. utilize

56. Jason's bossy character and his wish to _____ over others make him the least popular person among all.

Control is in the closest meaning to this word.

A. dominate   C. prevent

B. accommodate   D. segregate

53. 科學家正在研發具多重功用的機器人以提供服務來滿足所有使用者各種不同的需求。

Producing 的意思最接近於這個字。

A. **發展**　　　　C. 標記

B. 反對　　　　　D. 滅亡

54. 這名應徵者額外的語言技能和工作經驗必定可以使他增加被僱用的機會。

Add 的意思最接近於這個字。

A. 縮寫　　　　　C. 佔據

B. **增加**　　　　D. 抵抗

55. 為了降低動脈堵塞及心臟病發生的風險，人們最好遠離會導致血液中膽固醇提高的反式脂肪。

Decrease 的意思最接近於這個字。

A. **減少**　　　　C. 下結論

B. 累積　　　　　D. 利用

56. 傑森愛指使人的個性以及總是喜歡控制別人的作風，使他成為所有人當中最不受歡迎的一個。

Control 的意思最接近於這個字。

A. **統治**　　　　C. 預防

B. 容納　　　　　D. 隔離

答案　**53.** A　**54.** B　**55.** A　**56.** A

57. Due to the continuous bad selling condition, the company _____ that a certain percentage of the staff members had to be laid off.
Announced is in the closest meaning to this word.
A. cultivated   C. declared
B. migrated   D. submitted

58. The poor financial management of Mr. Smith's enterprise was responsible for his unfortunate _____ in the end.
Failure is in the closest meaning to this word.
A. achievement   C. innocence
B. recommendation   D. bankruptcy

59. It's essential for every global villager to keep it in mind that we all should undertake the _____ to protect the environment for our future generations.
Duty is in the closest meaning to this word.
A. structure   C. hospitality
B. obligation   D. irrigation

60. Dr. Martin Luther King Jr.'s _____ of non-violence in struggling against racial discrimination and segregation won him the utmost respect from the world.
Maintenance is in the closest meaning to this word.
A. shortcoming   C. probation
B. opportunity   D. advocacy

57. 由於不良的銷售狀況持續地發生，這家公司宣佈特定比例的職員必須被裁員。

Announced 的意思最接近於這個字。

  A. 培養   C. **宣佈**

  B. 遷徙   D. 投降

58. 企業不良的財政營運狀況導致史密斯先生最終不幸面臨破產。

Failure 的意思最接近於這個字。

  A. 成就   C. 無辜

  B. 推薦   D. **破產**

59. 每位地球村的居民必定要謹記在心：我們都應該為後代子孫承擔起保護環境的義務。

Duty 的意思最接近於這個字。

  A. 結構   C. 好客

  B. **義務**   D. 灌溉

60. 馬丁・路德・金恩博士在對抗種族歧視和隔離政策所倡導非暴力的方式為他贏得世人最崇高的敬意。

Maintenance 的意思最接近於這個字。

  A. 缺點   C. 緩刑

  B. 機會   D. **倡導**

答案 **57.** C   **58.** D   **59.** B   **60.** D

Part 1 同義字模擬試題

Part 2 填空題模擬試題

Part 3 聽、讀整合能力強化

模擬試題（六）

✏ Vocabulary in Context

61. Jeremy Lin _____ himself as a humble and prominent Asian American NBA player.
Differentiates is in the closest meaning to this word.
A. laments
C. installs
B. distinguishes
D. tolerates

62. To reduce the impact of global warming on humans, _____ researches and scientists all over the world are developing alternative energy.
Assets is in the closest meaning to this word.
A. equipment
C. prosecution
B. resources
D. assurances

63. The reckless truck driver, talking on the cell phone while driving, wasn't _____ of the approaching car and got crashed.
Conscious is in the closest meaning to this word.
A. iconic
C. aware
B. silent
D. complacent

64. All those present were bothered by the intruder, who both inappropriately dressed himself and rudely behaved on the solemn _____.
Circumstance is in the closest meaning to this word.
A. calamity
C. occasion
B. suburb
D. moderation

61. 林書豪以身為一名謙遜且傑出的美籍亞裔 NBA 球員獨樹一格。
Differentiates 的意思最接近於這個字。
A. 哀嘆　　　　　C. 安裝
B. **顯出特色**　　D. 忍受

62. 為了要減少全球暖化對人類所造成的衝擊，世界各地的研究學者和科學家正在研發替代能源。
Assets 的意思最接近於這個字。
A. 設備　　　　　C. 起訴
B. **資源**　　　　D. 保證

63. 這位粗心的卡車司機邊開車邊講手機，沒有意識到前來的車輛而撞車。
Conscious 的意思最接近於這個字。
A. 圖像的　　　　C. **有意識的**
B. 沉默的　　　　D. 自滿的

64. 所有出席這個莊重場合的人皆受到這位穿著不合宜且行為粗魯的入侵者的干擾。
Circumstance 的意思最接近於這個字。
A. 災難　　　　　C. **場合**
B. 郊區　　　　　D. 適度

答案　**61.** B　**62.** B　**63.** C　**64.** C

65. To fill the growing _____ for their merchandise, the workers of the factory were required to work overtime.
Need is in the closest meaning to this word.
A. discount   C. demand
B. notification   D. nomination

66. Though careful with the budget, with the soaring high living costs, Michael's expenses invariably _____ his income every month.
Surpassed is in the closest meaning to this word.
A. exceeded   C. conquered
B. subsidized   D. immigrated

67. Alexander Bell had a highly _____ mind. After making many years of experiments, in 1876, his "talking machine," the telephone, finally came out and changed people's lives.
Creative is in the closest meaning to this word.
A. cooperative   C. inventive
B. disastrous   D. reliable

68. Although Tom was the best player of the team, Coach Miller had to _____ him with another player because of his serious knee injury.
Substitute is in the closest meaning to this word.
A. predict   C. litter
B. replace   D. conflict

65. 為了要應付他們商品數量逐漸增加的需求，工廠員工被要求加班。
Need 的意思最接近於這個字。

A. 打折　　　　　C. **需求**

B. 通知　　　　　D. 提名

66. 雖然小心翼翼地做預算，但隨著生活費用的高升，麥可每個月必定入不敷出。

Surpassed 的意思最接近於這個字。

A. **超過**　　　　C. 征服

B. 補助　　　　　D. 遷入

67. 亞歷山大‧貝爾擁有高度發明的創意。經過多年實驗之後，在 1876 年，他那部"會講話的機器"，也就是電話，終於問世並且改變了人類的生活。

Creative 的意思最接近於這個字。

A. 合作的　　　　C. **發明的**

B. 毀滅的　　　　D. 可靠的

68. 儘管湯姆是球隊中最好的球員，由於他的膝蓋嚴重受傷，米勒教練不得不以另一名球員取代他。

Substitute 的意思最接近於這個字。

A. 預測　　　　　C. 亂丟

B. **取代**　　　　D. 衝突

答案　65. C　66. A　67. C　68. B

69. On Christmas, every household decorates their Christmas trees and the house will be _____ with the twinkling lights, adding warmth and joy to the atmosphere.
Bright is in the closest meaning to this word.
A. confident C. brilliant
B. stressful D. panoramic

70. As soon as the renowned company posted an advertisement of a position for a manager, a large number of qualified jobseekers _____ for the job.
Administered is in the closest meaning to this word.
A. applied C. monitored
B. disobeyed D. transferred

71. In different countries, all kinds of hand gestures _____ varied hints; thus, to avoid offending others, tourists had better look into them first.
Express is in the closest meaning to this word.
A. admire C. convey
B. stimulate D. reconfirm

72. It remains a mystery that just how certain people possessing the special ability to generate electricity should have the _____ power.
Unusual is in the closest meaning to this word.
A. harmful C. classical
B. unemployed D. extraordinary

69. 耶誕節時，每個家庭裝飾耶誕樹，房子因閃閃發亮的燈飾而明亮，增添了溫馨歡樂的氣氛。

Bright 的意思最接近於這個字。

A. 自信的　　　　C. **明亮的**
B. 有壓力的　　　D. 全景的

70. 這間聲譽卓越的公司一張貼徵求經理職位的廣告，大批符合資格的求職者前來申請這個工作。

Administered 的意思最接近於這個字。

A. **申請**　　　　C. 監督
B. 反抗　　　　　D. 移轉

71. 在不同的國家中，各種手勢傳達不同的暗示；因此，為了避免冒犯他人，觀光客最好事先做了解。

Express 的意思最接近於這個字。

A. 仰慕　　　　　C. **傳達**
B. 刺激　　　　　D. 再確定

72. 某些擁有產生電力能力的人士究竟是如何能夠具有此特殊的本領是一個謎。

Unusual 的意思最接近於這個字。

A. 傷害的　　　　C. 經典的
B. 失業的　　　　D. **非凡的**

答案　**69.** C　**70.** A　**71.** C　**72.** D

模擬試題（七）

UNIT 7

Vocabulary in Context

73. When writing his doctoral thesis, Frank made good use of the _____ facilities in the school library and finally got graduated with honors.

Obtainable is in the closest meaning to this word.

A. chaotic   C. religious

B. available   D. paradoxical

74. In _____, when asking someone for help while you travel in Europe, you may speak English. However, the local people will be much pleasant if you ask in their language.

Common is in the closest meaning to this word.

A. general   C. advance

B. memory   D. circulation

75. We are fortunate to live in an era of convenience and information. Through the far-reaching Internet, we can easily get _____ with the world.

Linked is in the closest meaning to this word.

A. connected   C. submerged

B. delayed   D. organized

76. Online shoppers always find themselves get attracted by the dazzling _____advertisements and increase the unnecessary spending.

Mercantile is in the closest meaning to this word.

A. vulnerable   C. commercial

B. idiomatic   D. reluctant

73. 法蘭克在寫博士論文時，善用學校圖書館裡可利用的設備，並在最後以優異的成績畢業。

Obtainable 的意思最接近於這個字。

A. 混亂的   C. 宗教的

B. **可利用的**   D. 自相矛盾的

74. 一般而言，在歐洲旅遊時，你可以使用英語向他人請求幫助。然而，假使你使用他們的語言，當地人會更樂於提供協助。

Common 的意思最接近於這個字。

A. **一般**   C. 預先

B. 記憶   D. 循環

75. 我們很幸運地生活在一個資訊便利的時代。經由無遠弗屆的網際網路，我們可以很輕易地和世界接軌。

Linked 的意思最接近於這個字。

A. **連結的**   C. 淹沒的

B. 延遲的   D. 組織的

76. 線上購物者發現自己經常會被炫目的商業廣告所吸引而增加不必要的消費。

Mercantile 的意思最接近於這個字。

A. 易受傷的   C. **商業的**

B. 慣用語的   D. 不情願的

答案 **73.** B   **74.** A   **75.** A   **76.** C

77. Though the Dutch painter, Vincent Van Gogh, had a miserable life all his life, he was _____ of as one of the most talented and the most influential artists in the world.
Thought is in the closest meaning to this word.
A. dismissed   C. considered
B. reflected   D. nurtured

78. According to medical researches, nuts are very _____ at lowering cholesterol levels and preventing heart and blood vessel diseases.
Effectual is in the closest meaning to this word.
A. redundant   C. compassionate
B. nimble   D. effective

79. DNA was _____ by a German scientist, Friedrich Miescher, in 1869. From the information in DNA, a lot about a human's family, health, and personality can be revealed.
Found is in the closest meaning to this word.
A. discovered   C. notified
B. preferred   D. interviewed

80. Pablo Picasso, probably the most important painter of the 20th century, _____ an enviable reputation for his outstanding artistic ability.
Obtained is in the closest meaning to this word.
A. compensated   C. acquired
B. forbade   D. subordinated

77. 雖然荷蘭畫家，文森・梵谷，這一生命運多舛，他仍被視為全世界最具天分且最具影響力的藝術家之一。
Thought 的意思最接近於這個字。
A. 解散　　　　　C. **認為**
B. 反射　　　　　D. 養育

78. 根據醫學研究，堅果在降低膽固醇以及預防心血管疾病方面非常有效果。
Effectual 的意思最接近於這個字。
A. 多餘的　　　　C. 同情的
B. 敏捷的　　　　D. **有效的**

79. DNA 是由德國科學家，弗雷德里希・米歇爾，在 1869 年所發現的。從 DNA 所呈現的訊息，可以充分了解一個人的家族血緣、健康狀況，以及人格特質。
Found 的意思最接近於這個字。
A. **發現**　　　　C. 通知
B. 寧願　　　　　D. 面試

80. 巴布羅・畢卡索可說是 20 世紀最重要的畫家，他以他傑出的藝術才能獲得令人仰慕的聲譽。
Obtained 的意思最接近於這個字。
A. 賠償　　　　　C. **獲得**
B. 禁止　　　　　D. 居次要地位

答案　**77.** C　**78.** D　**79.** A　**80.** C

81. With a strong _____ for childcare, Rebecca has devoted herself to teaching in a kindergarten and has done a great job.
Enthusiasm is in the closest meaning to this word.
A. complaint   C. tradition
B. passion   D. service

82. Mark made up his mind to be a doctor and worked hard for it. No hardness could stop him from _____ his goal.
Seeking is in the closest meaning to this word.
A. regretting   C. commemorating
B. pursuing   D. integrating

83. This brand of laptop has been selling well for it's _____, portable, and easy to operate.
Cheap is in the closest meaning to this word.
A. ambiguous   C. dialectic
B. weighty   D. inexpensive

84. You can of course contact a travel agency to make travel arrangements for you; one _____ to this is that you and your family can organize your own trip.
Choice is in the closest meaning to this word.
A. recipe   C. alternative
B. seclusion   D. depreciation

81. 蕾貝嘉對於照顧兒童有著強烈的熱忱，她一直致力於幼稚園的教學並且勝任稱職。

Enthusiasm 的意思最接近於這個字。

A. 抱怨 　　　　C. 傳統

B. 熱情 　　　D. 服務

82. 馬克下定決心並致力於成為一名醫生。沒有任何困難可以阻止他追求他的目標。

Seeking 的意思最接近於這個字。

A. 後悔 　　　　C. 紀念

B. 追求 　　　D. 融合

83. 這個品牌的筆電銷路一向不錯，因為它價格便宜、便於攜帶，並且易於操作。

Cheap 的意思最接近於這個字。

A. 模稜兩可的 　　C. 方言的

B. 沉重的 　　　　**D. 便宜的**

84. 你當然可以接洽旅行社為你做旅遊行程的安排；此外的另一選擇是你可以和你的家人共同籌畫你們自己的行程。

Choice 的意思最接近於這個字。

A. 食譜 　　　　　**C. 可供選擇的事物**

B. 隱居 　　　　　D. 貶值

答案　**81.** B　**82.** B　**83.** D　**84.** C

8
UNIT

模擬試題（八）

✎ Vocabulary in Context

85. The most _____ trip for the happy couple was the trip to Europe for their 10th Wedding Anniversary.
Memorable is in the closest meaning to this word.
A. routine
C. constant
B. unforgettable
D. subsequent

86. It's hard to _____ what life would be like if there were no water and electricity in the world.
Fancy is in the closest meaning to this word.
A. nourish
C. imagine
B. unlock
D. dismantle

87. Scientists have found that the music that Mozart composed and _____ has a miraculous healing and calming effect to its listeners.
Played is in the closest meaning to this word.
A. performed
C. desolated
B. exchanged
D. necessitated

88. Dealing with _____ from all sources is no easy task; however, to gain true happiness, it's worth making the efforts.
Stress is in the closest meaning to this word.
A. ecstasy
C. pressure
B. morality
D. transport

85. 對這對幸福的夫婦來説，最難忘的旅遊是歡慶十周年結婚紀念前往歐洲的那趟旅遊。

    Memorable 的意思最接近於這個字。

    A. 例行的　　　　C. 時常的

    B. 難忘的　　　D. 隨後的

86. 很難想像世界上假使沒有水和電，生活將會是什麼樣子。

    Fancy 的意思最接近於這個字。

    A. 提供養分　　　**C. 想像**

    B. 解開　　　　　D. 拆除

87. 科學家發現莫札特所創造和演奏的樂曲對於聽眾具有奇蹟般治療和鎮定的效果。

    Played 的意思最接近於這個字。

    A. 演奏　　　　C. 使荒涼

    B. 交換　　　　　D. 需要

88. 處理各種壓力不是件簡單的事；然而，為了獲得真正的快樂，努力是值得的。

    Stress 的意思最接近於這個字。

    A. 狂喜　　　　　**C. 壓力**

    B. 道德　　　　　D. 運輸

答案　**85.** B　**86.** C　**87.** A　**88.** C

89. The serial killer's bold and _____ murdering finally resulted in his being arrested and sentenced.

Ceaseless is in the closest meaning to this word.

A. worthwhile   C. tropical

B. continuous   D. contemporary

90. The methods of mass production and mass markets were first provided by the Industrial _____ in the 18th century, which in turn contributed to the development of international business.

Revolt is in the closest meaning to this word.

A. Fair   C. Engineering

B. Cooperation   D. Revolution

91. Richard was the "Workaholic" in his office because he always kept himself busy and was fully _____ in his work.

Occupied is in the closest meaning to this word.

A. engaged   C. signified

B. condensed   D. underwent

92. The Dinosaur Park in Canada has always been a _____ and popular tourist spot, where visitors can appreciate all kinds of dinosaur fossils.

Renowned is in the closest meaning to this word.

A. famous   C. notorious

B. delicious   D. subconscious

89. 這名連續殺人犯大膽且持續地犯案，終究導致他被逮捕並判刑。
Ceaseless 的意思最接近於這個字。
  A. 值得做的　　　C. 熱帶的
  B. 持續的　　　D. 當代的

90. 18 世紀的工業革命提供大規模生產的方式以及市場，進而促成國際商業的發展。
Revolt 的意思最接近於這個字。
  A. 展覽會　　　C. 工程學
  B. 合作　　　　**D. 革命**

91. 理察是他辦公室裡的「工作狂」，因為他總是十分忙碌並且全神貫注於他的工作。
Occupied 的意思最接近於這個字。
  A. 從事　　　C. 表示
  B. 濃縮　　　　D. 經歷

92. 加拿大的恐龍公園一向是著名並且受歡迎的觀光景點，訪客在這裡可以欣賞到各式各樣的恐龍化石。
Renowned 的意思最接近於這個字。
  A. 著名的　　　C. 惡名昭彰的
  B. 美味的　　　　D. 潛意識的

答案　**89.** B　**90.** D　**91.** A　**92.** A

93. Fanny studied and researched diligently and finally got _____ to her ideal graduate school.
Consented is in the closest meaning to this word.
A. admitted   C. perplexed
B. immigrated   D. resembled

94. It took Philip one whole month to _____ the long novel into one with only three chapters.
Shorten is in the closest meaning to this word.
A. wander   C. solicit
B. condense   D. forecast

95. Owing to the _____ resources, we must do our utmost to come up with practical measures for sustainable development.
Restricted is in the closest meaning to this word.
A. swift   C. marginal
B. limited   D. radioactive

96. _____, with the company of a new pet dog, Raymond recovered from the depression and the guiltiness of losing his old dog.
Progressively is in the closest meaning to this word.
A. Splendidly   C. Attractively
B. Previously   D. Gradually

93. 芬妮十分勤勉地讀書及做研究，最終錄取並進入她理想的研究所。
Consented 的意思最接近於這個字。
A. **錄取**　　　C. 困惑
B. 移民　　　　D. 相似

94. 菲力普花了整整一個月的時間把一本長篇小說濃縮成只有三個章節。
Shorten 的意思最接近於這個字。
A. 徘徊　　　　C. 請求
B. **濃縮**　　　D. 預測

95. 由於資源有限，我們必須盡最大的努力提出可供持續發展的實際措施。
Restricted 的意思最接近於這個字。
A. 迅速的　　　C. 邊緣的
B. **有限的**　　D. 放射性的

96. 逐漸地，有著新寵物狗的陪伴，雷蒙從失去原有的狗所引發的憂鬱和愧疚中恢復過來。
Progressively 的意思最接近於這個字。
A. 華麗地　　　C. 吸引人地
B. 先前地　　　D. **逐漸地**

答案　**93.** A　**94.** B　**95.** B　**96.** D

模擬試題（九）

UNIT 9

✏ Vocabulary in Context
MP3 009

97. In the action movie, the superheroes, with each of whom equipped with combating skills, finally won the victory with _____ forces.
Supreme is in the closest meaning to this word.
A. temporary   C. seasonal
B. dominant   D. fundamental

98. Undoubtedly, it is the parents that should strictly regulate their children not to watch TV programs that are too _____ in violence.
Lifelike is in the closest meaning to this word.
A. realistic   C. conventional
B. amiable   D. luxuriant

99. After transferring to the new company, Lucy could pleasantly work in a much more _____ and efficient way.
Adjustable is in the closest meaning to this word.
A. agricultural   C. flexible
B. uncertain   D. legitimate

100. As a safety policy against terroism, all passengers are _____ to undergo and pass the strict security check at the airport.
Demanded is in the closest meaning to this word.
A. compiled   C. worshipped
B. required   D. overestimated

58

97. 在這部動作片中，超級英雄們各個身懷絕技，最終以絕佳優勢贏得勝利。

Supreme 的意思最接近於這個字。

A. 暫時的 　　　　 C. 季節的

B. **優勢的** 　　　　 D. 基本的

98. 無疑地，父母親應該嚴格規範孩童不要觀看過於暴力寫實的電視節目。

Lifelike 的意思最接近於這個字。

A. **寫實的** 　　　　 C. 傳統的

B. 和藹的 　　　　 D. 繁茂的

99. 露西在轉任到新公司後，可以很愉快地以更加彈性而且有效率的方式工作。

Adjustable 的意思最接近於這個字。

A. 農業的 　　　　 C. **彈性的**

B. 不確定的 　　　　 D. 合法正當的

100. 基於對抗恐怖主義的安全政策，所有的乘客被要求接受並且通過機場嚴格的安全檢查。

Demanded 的意思最接近於這個字。

A. 編纂 　　　　 C. 崇拜

B. **要求** 　　　　 D. 高估

答案 **97.** B 　 **98.** A 　 **99.** C 　 **100.** B

101. What the general public expects from the government is a
_____ economic development that it is supposed to achieve.
Steady is in the closest meaning to this word.
A. changeable
C. stable
B. alcoholic
D. waterproof

102. A lot of celebrities dressed up and attended the party tonight to support the charity campaign that was _____ by the association.
Started is in the closest meaning to this word.
A. amplified
C. launched
B. prolonged
D. twinkled

103. The news reporter purchased the newest laptop computer _____ for the purpose of covering instant news.
Particularly is in the closest meaning to this word.
A. affectionately
C. gloriously
B. narrowly
D. specifically

104. Doctors warned people against the long _____ to the burning sunlight, which might easily cause skin cancer.
Uncovering is in the closest meaning to this word.
A. reliability
C. exposure
B. dedication
D. negligence

101. 一般民眾對於政府的期許是一個理當由它所達成穩定的經濟發展。
    Steady 的意思最接近於這個字。
    A. 易變的　　　　C. **穩定的**
    B. 含酒精的　　　D. 防水的

102. 許多名流盛裝出席今晚的宴會來支持由協會所發起的慈善活動。
    Started 的意思最接近於這個字。
    A. 放大　　　　　C. **發起**
    B. 延長　　　　　D. 閃爍

103. 這名新聞記者為了採訪即時新聞特地購買了最新型的筆記型電腦。
    Particularly 的意思最接近於這個字。
    A. 關愛地　　　　C. 輝煌地
    B. 狹隘地　　　　D. **特別地**

104. 醫生警告人們不要長時間曝曬在熾熱的陽光下，因為這樣容易罹患
    皮膚癌。
    Uncovering 的意思最接近於這個字。
    A. 可靠　　　　　C. **曝曬**
    B. 奉獻　　　　　D. 輕忽

答案　101. C　102. C　103. D　104. C

105. President Barack Obama, the first African-American president has been admired worldwide for his _____ achievements in both domestic and foreign affairs.
Prominent is in the closest meaning to this word.
A. conceited   C. short-sighted
B. identical   D. outstanding

106. It's amazing and puzzling how the ancient Egyptians could have had the ability to _____ the Great Pyramids of Giza.
Build is in the closest meaning to this word.
A. construct   C. predict
B. whisper   D. intervene

107. Oliver is at present a resident doctor in the hospital his father _____ and plans to take over his father's business in the future.
Founded is in the closest meaning to this word.
A. appealed   C. smuggled
B. established   D. broadcast

108. Patrick has been under _____ pressure recently as he has to make an immediate decision on whether to work in the hometown or to accept the challenging position overseas.
Forceful is in the closest meaning to this word.
A. reputable   C. intense
B. climatic   D. merciful

105. 巴拉克‧歐巴馬總統是首位非裔美籍的總統，以他在內政及外交方面傑出的成就為世人所崇拜。

Prominent 的意思最接近於這個字。

A. 自負的　　　　C. 短視的

B. 相同的　　　　**D. 傑出的**

106. 人們對於古代埃及人竟然有能力建造吉薩的大金塔感到驚奇而且困惑。

Build 的意思最接近於這個字。

A. **建造**　　　　C. 預測

B. 耳語　　　　D. 干預

107. 奧利佛目前在他父親所建立的醫院裡擔任住院醫師，並且計劃在未來接管父親的事業。

Founded 的意思最接近於這個字。

A. 吸引　　　　C. 走私

B. **建立**　　　　D. 轉播

108. 派翠克最近身處於極大的壓力之下，因為他必須要盡快決定留在家鄉工作或是接受國外具挑戰性的職務。

Forceful 的意思最接近於這個字。

A. 聲譽好的　　　**C. 強烈的**

B. 氣候的　　　　D. 仁慈的

答案　105. D　106. A　107. B　108. C

10 UNIT

模擬試題（十）

✏️ Vocabulary in Context

MP3 010

109. The ancient Machu Picchu used to be a summer resort for Incan emperors and their _____ family.
Royal is in the closest meaning to this word.
A. abusive C. imperial
B. tempting D. contemplating

110. All the students unwillingly _____ the cancellation of the field trip because of the approaching typhoon.
Accepted is in the closest meaning to this word.
A. deserted C. symbolized
B. received D. prolonged

111. The publicity campaign did much to _____ the new product, promoting its unexpected big sale.
Advertise is in the closest meaning to this word.
A. anticipate C. depopulate
B. retire D. popularize

112. Donald adopted practical and clever marketing _____ and earned great profits for his company.
Skills is in the closest meaning to this word.
A. balances C. techniques
B. supposition D. coincidence

109. 馬丘比丘古城過去曾經是印加國王和他們的皇室家族避暑的地點。
Royal 的意思最接近於這個字。

A. 虐待的　　　　C. **皇室的**
B. 誘人的　　　　D. 深思的

110. 由於颱風即將來臨，所有的學生不情願地接受戶外教學的取消。
Accepted 的意思最接近於這個字。

A. 遺棄　　　　C. 象徵
B. **接受**　　　　D. 延長

111. 這項宣傳活動對於提升新產品的知名度有很大的幫助，促成了意想不到的大賣。
Advertise 的意思最接近於這個字。

A. 預期　　　　C. 減少人口
B. 退休　　　　D. **受歡迎**

112. 唐納採用實際而且靈活的行銷技巧為他的公司賺取大量的利潤。
Skills 的意思最接近於這個字。

A. 均衡　　　　C. **技巧**
B. 猜測　　　　D. 巧合

答案　**109.** C　　**110.** B　　**111.** D　　**112.** C

65

113. Besides the strict enforcement of laws against drunk driving, our government should conduct public education to alert people to the dangers of drunk driving to _____ their safety.

Assure is in the closest meaning to this word.

A. ensure   C. switch

B. overload   D. undermine

114. The candidate suffered a serious setback when the newsweekly _____ a series of disgraceful scandals about his family.

Uncovered is in the closest meaning to this word.

A. flourished   C. revealed

B. paraded   D. discouraged

115. It was irresponsible of Miss Hope to make the serious _____ against Carl that he had stolen her cell phone before she had any positive proof.

Charge is in the closest meaning to this word.

A. occupation   C. inhabitant

B. harassment   D. accusation

116. Since the merchandise of his company has superior quality and famous branding, Sam could easily achieve successful sales and _____.

Advancement is in the closest meaning to this word.

A. treatment   C. convenience

B. promotion   D. depiction

113. 除了取締酒駕法律嚴格的執行，我們的政府應該實施大眾教育使民眾警覺酒駕的危險以確保自身的安全。
    Assure 的意思最接近於這個字。
    A. **確保**　　　C. 轉換
    B. 超載　　　　D. 破壞

114. 當新聞週刊揭露一連串有關於他的家族丟臉的醜聞時，這名候選人遭受嚴重的挫折。
    Uncovered 的意思最接近於這個字。
    A. 茂盛　　　　C. **揭露**
    B. 遊行　　　　D. 氣餒

115. 霍普老師非常不負責任，因為她在還沒有任何證據之前就嚴正地指控卡爾偷竊她的手機。
    Charge 的意思最接近於這個字。
    A. 職業　　　　C. 居民
    B. 騷擾　　　　D. **指控**

116. 由於山姆公司的商品具有優異的品質以及著名的品牌，他可以輕易地達成成功的販售及促銷。
    Advancement 的意思最接近於這個字。
    A. 治療　　　　C. 便利
    B. **促銷**　　　D. 描繪

答案　113. A　114. C　115. D　116. B

117. Due to her thoughtful personality and language capability, Lydia was fully qualified as a competent flight _____.
Stewardess is in the closest meaning to this word.

A. rebel   C. attendant

B. detective   D. principal

118. Mother Teresa's lifelong devotion to the welfare of people and the advocacy of humanity won worldwide _____ and was awarded the Nobel Peace Prize in 1979.
Acknowledgement is in the closest meaning to this word.

A. trifle   C. appointment

B. permanence   D. recognition

119. It was naïve of Anna to _____ that everyone would support her proposal wholeheartedly.
Suppose is in the closest meaning to this word.

A. assume   C. renovate

B. compose   D. overwhelm

120. His making a scene of trifles in the middle of the party _____ not only himself but his family present on the scene.
Disgraced is in the closest meaning to this word.

A. amused   C. dedicated

B. insulted   D. reproached

117. 由於她善解人意的個性及語言的能力，莉迪亞有充分的資格成為勝任的空服員。

Stewardess 的意思最接近於這個字。

A. 反叛者　　　C. **服務員**

B. 偵探　　　　D. 校長

118. 德蕾莎修女因一生奉獻於人類的福祉以及人道主義的倡導而贏得世人的讚譽，並且在 1979 年獲頒諾貝爾和平獎。

Acknowledgement 的意思最接近於這個字。

A. 瑣事　　　　C. 任命

B. 永久　　　　D. **讚譽**

119. 安娜過於天真地認為每個人都會全心地支持她的提案。

Suppose 的意思最接近於這個字。

A. **假定**　　　C. 整修

B. 組成　　　　D. 壓倒

120. 他在宴會中為小事大吵大鬧，不僅侮辱自己也使得在場的家人蒙羞。

Disgraced 的意思最接近於這個字。

A. 取悅　　　　C. 致力

B. **侮辱**　　　D. 責備

答案　**117.** C　**118.** D　**119.** A　**120.** B

模擬試題（十一）

Vocabulary in Context MP3 011

121. Little did we expect that the minor misunderstanding between the couple should have _____ caused them to break up.
Unexpectedly is in the closest meaning to this word.
A. gracefully   C. abundantly
B. luxuriously   D. dramatically

122. It was a _____ belief in the past that after the appearance of a comet, which was regarded as an omen, great disasters and tragedies might occur.
General is in the closest meaning to this word.
A. common   C. passionate
B. solitary   D. luminous

123. Those naughty students were insistently requested to make a(n) _____ of their misbehavior, or they might receive a severe punishment.
Alteration is in the closest meaning to this word.
A. efficiency   C. separation
B. mistakes   D. corrections

124. People all over the world used to view the United States as a land of golden _____ and tried their luck by emigrating there.

Chance is in the closest meaning to this word.

A. warehouse
C. remedy
B. opportunity
D. derivation

121. 我們一點都沒料到這對情侶間小小的誤會竟然會戲劇性地導致他們分手。

Unexpectedly 的意思最接近於這個字。

A. 優雅地
C. 豐富地
B. 奢華地
D. 戲劇性地

122. 在過去，人們普遍地相信在被視為是凶兆的彗星出現後，巨大的災難和悲劇可能會發生。

General 的意思最接近於這個字。

A. **普遍的**
C. 熱情的
B. 孤單的
D. 發光的

123. 那些頑皮的學生一再地被要求改正他們不良的行為，否則他們可能將得接受嚴厲的處分。

Alteration 的意思最接近於這個字。

A. 效率
C. 分開
B. 錯誤
D. 修正

124. 在過去，世界各地的人們把美國視為是一個充滿絕佳機會的國度因而移民到那裏去開創契機。

Chance 的意思最接近於這個字。

A. 倉庫
C. 治療藥方
B. **機會**
D. 起源

答案 **121.** D **122.** A **123.** D **124.** B

Part 1 同義字模擬試題

Part 2 填空題模擬試題

Part 3 聽、讀整合能力強化

125. Carlos bought an apartment near the MRT station as he considered it _____ and time-saving for him to commute by MRT.
Handy is in the closest meaning to this word.
A. convenient
C. annoying
B. slight
D. theoretical

126. According to TV reports, the sending out of the _____ gas and fumes of the factory might be the cause of the serious sickness of the residents.
Poisonous is in the closest meaning to this word.
A. harmless
C. toxic
B. spacious
D. architectural

127. In America, young people will often move out and live an _____ life when they turn eighteen or go to college.
Autonomous is in the closest meaning to this word.
A. anxious
C. undermined
B. energetic
D. independent

128. _____, the speedy passenger ship hit on an iceberg and got crashed, resulting in heavy casualties.
Unluckily is in the closest meaning to this word.
A. Gratefully
C. Unfortunately
B. Collectively
D. Mutually

125. 卡洛斯在捷運站附近買了一間公寓，因為他認為坐捷運通勤既方便又節省時間。

Handy 的意思最接近於這個字。

A. **便利的**　　　C. 煩人的
B. 輕微的　　　D. 理論的

126. 根據電視新聞報導，這座工廠排放出的有毒氣體和煙霧可能是導致居民罹患嚴重疾病的主因。

Poisonous 的意思最接近於這個字。

A. 無害的　　　　C. **有毒的**
B. 寬敞的　　　　D. 建築的

127. 在美國，當年輕人到了十八歲或是上大學的時候，他們經常會搬離家庭並且過著獨立的生活。

Autonomous 的意思最接近於這個字。

A. 焦慮的　　　　C. 破壞的
B. 有活力的　　　D. **獨立的**

128. 很不幸地，疾馳而行的客輪撞上冰山撞毀，因而導致慘重的傷亡。

Unluckily 的意思最接近於這個字。

A. 感激地　　　　C. **不幸地**
B. 集體地　　　　D. 相互地

答案　125. A　126. C　127. D　128. C

129. The method of trial and _____ helped Mrs. Cooper a lot in her raising the three children.
Mistake is in the closest meaning to this word.
A. error   C. refund
B. contract   D. notification

130. Owing to economic recession, Mr. Norman's company met with the dramatic plunge in _____ and finally went bankrupt.
Earnings is in the closest meaning to this word.
A. beverage   C. equality
B. profits   D. findings

131. The American singer and song writer, Bob Dylan, gained _____ prestige by winning the 2016 Nobel Prize in Literature for his achievements in creating new poetic expressions within the great American song tradition.
Global is in the closest meaning to this word.
A. obscure   C. tribal
B. functional   D. international

132. Traveling a lot can be of great _____ to young people in broadening their horizons.
Advantage is in the closest meaning to this word.
A. morale   C. benefit
B. ailment   D. regularity

129. 「嘗試錯誤」的方法在庫柏太太撫育三個孩子方面有極大的幫助。
Mistake 的意思最接近於這個字。

    A. **錯誤**　　　　C. 退款
    B. 合約　　　　　D. 通知

130. 由於經濟不景氣，諾曼先生的公司遭逢利潤銳減的窘境，最終宣告破產。
Earnings 的意思最接近於這個字。

    A. 飲料　　　　　C. 平等
    B. **利潤**　　　　D. 發現

131. 美國歌手兼作曲家，巴比・狄倫，由於在偉大的美國歌曲傳統中注入創新詩意表達的成就而獲頒 2016 年諾貝爾文學獎，並因此贏得國際盛讚。
Global 的意思最接近於這個字。

    A. 模糊的　　　　C. 部落的
    B. 功能的　　　　D. **國際的**

132. 經常旅遊對於年輕人拓展視野具有很大的益處。
Advantage 的意思最接近於這個字。

    A. 士氣　　　　　C. **利益**
    B. 疾病　　　　　D. 規則性

 答案 129. A　130. B　131. D　132. C

模擬試題（十二）

✎ Vocabulary in Context

MP3 012

133. Andrew had a natural talent for learning and playing all kinds of musical _____, and he formed a rock band of his own when entering college.
Devices is in the closest meaning to this word.
A. animation   C. substitute
B. gestures   D. instruments

134. Due to the reddish coloring from the iron oxide on its _____, Mars is often referred to as the "Red Planet".
Exterior is in the closest meaning to this word.
A. surface   C. carpet
B. galaxy   D. maintenance

135. The corporation planned to establish chain stores all over the world and made great efforts to look for superior and _____ store managers.
Trustworthy is in the closest meaning to this word.
A. absent-minded   C. reliable
B. sanitary   D. descriptive

136. To achieve immortality and enjoy the afterlife, the ancient Egyptian pharaohs were mummified after their death to _____ their bodies from decaying.
Stop is in the closest meaning to this word.
A. abandon   C. celebrate
B. prevent   D. stipulate

133. 安德魯有學習和演奏各種樂器的天份，一上大學他就組了一支他自己的搖滾樂團。

Devices 的意思最接近於這個字。

A. 動畫   C. 替代品

B. 手勢   **D. 儀器**

134. 由於來自於星球表面的氧化鐵而形成紅色色澤，火星經常被稱為「紅色星球」。

Exterior 的意思最接近於這個字。

A. **表面**   C. 地毯

B. 銀河   D. 維修

135. 這家公司計畫在全世界建立連鎖店，因而努力尋找優秀且可靠的分店經理。

Trustworthy 的意思最接近於這個字。

A. 心不在焉的   **C. 可信賴的**

B. 衛生的   D. 描述的

136. 為了追求不朽以及享受來生，古埃及法老在死後被製作成木乃伊以防止遺體腐化。

Stop 的意思最接近於這個字。

A. 遺棄   C. 慶祝

B. **防止**   D. 規定

答案   **133.** D   **134.** A   **135.** C   **136.** B

137. The factory was forced to slow down its manufacturing speed after parts of its _____ apparatus went wrong.
Machine-operated is in the closest meaning to this word.
A. artistic
C. mechanical
B. symbolic
D. therapeutic

138. What is great about Bill Gates is that he is not only a successful _____ but a person dedicated to his ideals of making the world better by working for charitable causes.
Businessman is in the closest meaning to this word.
A. critic
C. publisher
B. narrator
D. entrepreneur

139. In the class reunion, we could hardly _____ Henry, who has changed a lot in appearance over the past ten years.
Identify is in the closest meaning to this word.
A. coax
C. inspect
B. recognize
D. enlighten

140. It's rather a pity that man _____ little on what he has but craves much for what he doesn't own.
Values is in the closest meaning to this word.
A. explains
C. tolerates
B. mingles
D. appreciates

137. 這座工廠在它部份的機械設備出狀況後，被迫放慢製造的速度。
Machine-operated 的意思最接近於這個字。
　A. 藝術的　　　　C. **機械的**
　B. 象徵的　　　　D. 有療效的

138. 比爾蓋茲了不起的地方在於他不僅是一名成功的企業家，並且是一
名致力於藉由從事慈善事業而使得這個世界更美好的理念的人。
Businessman 的意思最接近於這個字。
　A. 評論家　　　　C. 出版商
　B. 敘事者　　　　D. **企業家**

139. 在同學會中，我們幾乎認不出亨利了，因為他的外表在過去十年來
改變很多。
Identify 的意思最接近於這個字。
　A. 哄騙　　　　C. 檢查
　B. **認得**　　　　D. 啟蒙

140. 人們不珍惜他們所擁有的反而去過度渴望他們所沒有的東西是件令
人相當遺憾的事。
Values 的意思最接近於這個字。
　A. 說明　　　　C. 忍受
　B. 混和　　　　D. **賞識**

Part 1 同義字模擬試題

Part 2 填空題模擬試題

Part 3 聽、讀整合能力強化

答案　**137.** C　**138.** D　**139.** B　**140.** D

141. The notorious mayor, who committed bribery and embezzlement, finally handed in his _____ and was put in jail.
Quitting is in the closest meaning to this word.
A. thesis   C. resignation
B. measurement   D. disapproval

142. To _____ a higher level of education is vital to getting better employment and fairer salaries in the future.
Receive is in the closest meaning to this word.
A. obtain   C. inquire
B. promise   D. exaggerate

143. Talking too loudly on a cell phone may cause disturbance to people around you, _____ in a cinema.
Particularly is in the closest meaning to this word.
A. especially   C. potentially
B. consequently   D. righteously

144. To achieve the sustainability of the earth and humans, it's essential that we cherish and conserve the _____ natural ecosystems.
Undeveloped is in the closest meaning to this word.
A. doubtful   C. refundable
B. unexploited   D. communicative

141. 因犯下賄賂及盜用公款罪行而聲名狼藉的市長最後的結局是遞交辭呈並且被關入監獄裡。

Quitting 的意思最接近於這個字。

A. 論文　　　　　C. **辭職**
B. 測量　　　　　D. 不贊同

142. 獲得較高學位對於日後要取得較佳的工作及較高的薪水是很關鍵的。

Receive 的意思最接近於這個字。

A. **獲得**　　　　C. 詢問
B. 允諾　　　　　D. 誇大

143. 手機講太大聲可能會對你週遭的人造成困擾，尤其是在電影院裡的時候。

Particularly 的意思最接近於這個字。

A. **尤其**　　　　C. 潛在地
B. 結果　　　　　D. 正直地

144. 為了要達成地球和人類永續的生存，我們必須要珍惜並保護未開發的自然生態系統。

Undeveloped 的意思最接近於這個字。

A. 可疑的　　　　C. 可退款的
B. **未開發的**　　D. 溝通的

答案　**141.** C　**142.** A　**143.** A　**144.** B

 模擬試題（十三）

✎ Vocabulary in Context

MP3 013

145. Mr. Goodman enjoyed collecting the _____ Chinese art and antiques; he even opened an antique shop for his hobby.
Old is in the closest meaning to this word.
A. optimistic   C. ancient
B. venomous   D. supernatural

146. At the embarrassing moment, Anthony had a hard time finding _____ words to express his apology.
Proper is in the closest meaning to this word.
A. fragrant   C. proficient
B. suitable   D. antisocial

147. In _____ days, making proper health management is essential since health is the foundation of success and happiness.
Contemporary is in the closest meaning to this word.
A. modern   C. attractive
B. justifiable   D. prehistoric

148. As long as you make the _____, the department store counter will consent to allow a full refund of the amount paid.
Demand is in the closest meaning to this word.
A. ancestor   C. performance
B. flare   D. request

145. 古德曼先生喜愛收集古代中國藝術品和古董；他甚至因為這項嗜好開了一家古董店。
Old 的意思最接近於這個字。
A. 樂觀的　　　　C. **古代的**
B. 有毒的　　　　D. 超自然的

146. 在尷尬的那一瞬間，安東尼找不出貼切的話來表達他的歉意。
Proper 的意思最接近於這個字。
A. 芳香的　　　　C. 精通的
B. **適合的**　　　D. 反社會的

147. 就今日來説，由於健康是成功以及快樂的基礎，做好適當的健康管理是必要的。
Contemporary 的意思最接近於這個字。
A. **現代的**　　　C. 吸引人的
B. 有理由的　　　D. 史前的

148. 只要你提出要求，百貨公司櫃台會同意給予退還全部的付款。
Demand 的意思最接近於這個字。
A. 祖先　　　　　C. 表演
B. 閃光　　　　　D. **要求**

答案　145. C　146. B　147. A　148. D

149. It's _____ for people to yearn for longevity and scientists who have been working on ways of lengthening mankind's life span.

Normal is in the closest meaning to this word.

A. natural   C. impulsive
B. sociable   D. legitimate

150. The painful bothering and torments to celebrities and the _____ are the endless pursuit and photographing of the paparazzi.

Nobles is in the closest meaning to this word.

A. guardians   C. royalty
B. minority   D. artists

151. The brutal man committed serious crimes out of impulse; _____, he was sentenced to life imprisonment and was deprived of his civil rights.

Consequently is in the closest meaning to this word.

A. firstly   C. previously
B. however   D. therefore

152. It's generally believed that during the fourth century B.C., Alexander the Great _____ the arrival of perfume in Greece.

Presented is in the closest meaning to this word.

A. wrinkled   C. radiated
B. meditated   D. introduced

149. 人們渴望長壽是很自然的，而科學家正致力於尋找延長人類壽命的方法。

Normal 的意思最接近於這個字。

A. **自然的**　　　C. 衝動的

B. 擅長交際的　　D. 合法的

150. 名流和皇室成員痛苦的困擾及折磨在於狗仔隊永無止盡的跟蹤和拍照。

Nobles 的意思最接近於這個字。

A. 監護人　　　　C. **皇室成員**

B. 少數民族　　　D. 藝術家

151. 這個殘暴的人因衝動犯下嚴重的罪行；因此，他被判處終身監禁並且被剝奪公民權。

Consequently 的意思最接近於這個字。

A. 首先　　　　　C. 先前地

B. 然而　　　　　D. **因此**

152. 一般人相信在西元前第四世紀期間，亞歷山大大帝把香水引進至希臘。

Presented 的意思最接近於這個字。

A. 弄皺　　　　　C. 輻射

B. 沉思　　　　　D. **介紹**

答案　149. A　150. C　151. D　152. D

153. The extraordinary director, Ang Lee, has won himself an international _____ for his amazingly unique ways of directing films.
Fame is in the closest meaning to this word.
A. conservation   C. reputation
B. heritage   D. program

154. Out of pity, Rick _____ the old man who seemed to have lost his way to the police station and helped him return home.
Escorted is in the closest meaning to this word.
A. distorted   C. idolized
B. accompanied   D. supervised

155. Recently, a team of scientists, teachers, and students went on an _____ to explore some of the wonders of the Amazon Rainforest.
Journey is in the closest meaning to this word.
A. expedition   C. isolation
B. orchestra   D. unemployment

156. The board of directors announced several measures to minimize the problem to a more _____ level.
Controllable is in the closest meaning to this word.
A. opposing   C. casual
B. diplomatic   D. manageable

153. 卓越的李安導演因其令人驚嘆獨特的導演方式而贏得國際聲譽。
Fame 的意思最接近於這個字。

A. 保存   C. **聲望**

B. 遺產   D. 節目

154. 出自於同情，瑞克陪伴那位似乎迷路的老先生到警局並協助他返家。
Escorted 的意思最接近於這個字。

A. 扭曲   C. 崇拜

B. **伴隨**   D. 監督

155. 最近，一支由科學家、教師，以及學生組成的隊伍進行遠征去探索亞馬遜河熱帶雨林區的一些奇景。
Journey 的意思最接近於這個字。

A. **遠征**   C. 孤立

B. 管弦樂隊   D. 失業

156. 董事會宣佈數項措施來把問題降低到比較能應付的程度。
Controllable 的意思最接近於這個字。

A. 對立的   C. 隨意的

B. 外交的   D. **可處理的**

答案 **153.** C   **154.** B   **155.** A   **156.** D

模擬試題（十四）

✎ Vocabulary in Context
MP3 014

157. The admirable NBA basketball players are not only
_____ in their basketball skills but passionate and
generous in supporting charity work.
Well-trained is in the closest meaning to this word.
A. different   C. territorial
B. antisocial   D. professional

158. Though separated far apart, Melissa still maintained regular
_____ with her best friend these years.
Letter-writing is in the closest meaning to this word.
A. landscape   C. correspondence
B. poverty   D. temptation

159. Her elaborate presentation and smooth use of the
PowerPoint slides gave the _____ that she was well-
prepared and organized.
Feeling is in the closest meaning to this word.
A. cultivation   C. possession
B. impression   D. reservation

160. Due to _____ serious delays of shipment, the
company decided to ask for compensation or even a full
refund.
Many is in the closest meaning to this word.
A. numerous   C. scarce
B. logical   D. observant

157. 令人欽佩的 NBA 籃球球星不僅專業於他們的籃球技巧，並且熱情慷慨地支持慈善工作。
Well-trained 的意思最接近於這個字。
A. 不同的　　　　C. 領土的
B. 反社會的　　**D. 專業的**

158. 儘管相隔遙遠，梅莉莎這些年來仍然持續地和她最要好的朋友保持定期的通信。
Letter-writing 的意思最接近於這個字。
A. 風景　　　　**C. 通信**
B. 貧窮　　　　D. 誘惑

159. 她詳盡的報告以及流暢的簡報運用給予人們她事前準備充分並且條理分明的印象。
Feeling 的意思最接近於這個字。
A. 栽培　　　　C. 擁有
B. 印象　　　D. 預約

160. 由於多次貨物運送的嚴重延遲，這家公司決定要求索賠或甚至全額退款。
Many 的意思最接近於這個字。
A. 許多的　　C. 稀少的
B. 合邏輯的　　D. 善於觀察的

答案 **157.** D　**158.** C　**159.** B　**160.** A

161. Ralph got fired this month because his performance failed to reach the required _____; however, he planned to start all over again.
Criteria is in the closest meaning to this word.

A. publication   C. expansion
B. standard   D. trademark

162. As soon as Steven got his year-end bonus, he purchased a highly functional digital camera that could adjust _____.
Spontaneously is in the closest meaning to this word.

A. constructively   C. irrelevantly
B. gradually   D. automatically

163. The _____ cars shown in the International Car Fair attracted lots of car fans all over the world to appreciate.
Antique is in the closest meaning to this word.

A. pointed   C. vintage
B. accurate   D. sympathetic

164. Owing to generation gap, modern parents find it more and more difficult to _____ with their children.
Link is in the closest meaning to this word.

A. bewilder   C. project
B. exempt   D. communicate

161. 勞夫由於表現未達到要求的標準而在這個月遭到解雇；然而，他計畫全部重新開始。

Criteria 的意思最接近於這個字。

A. 出版　　　　C. 擴張

B. 標準　　　D. 商標

162. 史蒂芬一拿到年終獎金就去購買具有自動調節功能高度實用的數位相機。

Spontaneously 的意思最接近於這個字。

A. 建設性地　　　C. 無關地

B. 逐漸地　　　**D. 自動地**

163. 國際車展中陳列展示的古董車吸引許多世界各地的車迷慕名前來觀賞。

Antique 的意思最接近於這個字。

A. 尖銳的　　　**C. 古董的**

B. 正確的　　　D. 同情的

164. 由於代溝，現代的父母覺得越來越難和他們的孩子溝通。

Link 的意思最接近於這個字。

A. 困惑　　　　C. 投射

B. 免除　　　　**D. 溝通**

答案　**161.** B　**162.** D　**163.** C　**164.** D

165. The _____ expressions the professor used made it easier for the students to comprehend the difficult theories.

Condensed is in the closest meaning to this word.

A. simplified   C. desolate
B. arbitrary   D. nominal

166. The real estate prices brought up by rich investors recently have become hardly _____, especially to young people with low income.

Buyable is in the closest meaning to this word.

A. radical   C. unified
B. affordable   D. economical

167. The police tried to find the true murderer by _____ the suspects one by one through investigation.

Excluding is in the closest meaning to this word.

A. deceiving   C. overlapping
B. standardizing   D. eliminating

168. The heavy casualties on the superhighway last weekend resulted from the serious chain _____ among seven cars, accompanied by terrifying car-burning afterward.

Smashing is in the closest meaning to this word.

A. exception   C. collision
B. participation   D. reconciliation

165. 這位教授所使用簡化的解釋用語讓學生比較容易理解困難的理論。
Condensed 的意思最接近於這個字。
A. **簡化的**　　　C. 荒涼的
B. 獨斷的　　　　D. 名義上的

166. 近日由富有的投資者所帶動提高的房地產價格超出人們所能負擔，
尤其是對低薪的年輕人而言。
Buyable 的意思最接近於這個字。
A. 徹底的　　　　C. 統一的
B. **負擔得起的**　D. 節約的

167. 警方經由調查一一排除嫌疑犯試著去找出真正的兇手。
Excluding 的意思最接近於這個字。
A. 欺騙　　　　　C. 重疊
B. 標準化　　　　D. **排除**

168. 上週末在高速公路上的慘重傷亡肇因於七部車嚴重的連環追撞，伴
隨著後續恐怖的火燒車意外。
Smashing 的意思最接近於這個字。
A. 例外　　　　　C. **碰撞**
B. 參加　　　　　D. 和解

答案　**161.** A　**162.** B　**163.** D　**164.** C

模擬試題（十五）

Vocabulary in Context

MP3 015

169. The team going on the journey of exploration into the Brazilian tropical jungles _____ professors, researchers, and scientists.
Included is in the closest meaning to this word.
A. consisted of   C. worshipped
B. scattered   D. prohibited

170. The sample was observed carefully under _____ of 1,000 times their actual size through the powerful microscope.
Enlargement is in the closest meaning to this word.
A. projection   C. destruction
B. exclusion   D. magnification

171. According to archaeologists, the _____ of the Stonehenge in Southern England was originally to serve as an observatory and an astronomical calendar.
Building is in the closest meaning to this word.
A. disillusion   C. construction
B. prevalence   D. significance

172. After working in the company for ten years, Joseph decided to quit the job owing to the _____ of his enduring the heavy workload.

Limitation is in the closest meaning to this word.

A. serenity   C. charity

B. extremity   D. regularity

169. 這支前往巴西熱帶叢林考察的隊伍是由教授、研究人員，以及科學家所組成的。

Included 的意思最接近於這個字。

A. **組成**   C. 崇拜

B. 分散   D. 禁止

170. 這份樣本是透過放大 1000 倍於實物的高倍率顯微鏡加以仔細觀察的。

Enlargement 的意思最接近於這個字。

A. 投射   C. 毀壞

B. 排除   D. **放大**

171. 根據考古學家的說法，建造英國南方巨石陣原先的目的是用作天文觀測台以及天文曆法的功用。

Building 的意思最接近於這個字。

A. 幻滅   C. **建造**

B. 流行   D. 意義

172. 約瑟夫在這家公司工作十年後決定要辭職，因為他對於沉重工作負擔的忍耐已經到極限了。

Limitation 的意思最接近於這個字。

A. 寧靜   C. 慈善

B. **極端**   D. 規則性

答案 **169.** A   **170.** D   **171.** C   **172.** B

173. With his smooth body language, the salesman successfully _____ the operation of the kitchen appliances.
Displayed is in the closest meaning to this word.
A. cultivated   C. proclaimed
B. smuggled   D. demonstrated

174. It's odd that some people should be able to make accurate _____ about the future happening. They even claimed to have seen those incidents in person in their dreams.
Forecasts is in the closest meaning to this word.
A. expeditions   C. predictions
B. temptation   D. generation

175. The distant _____ of the Pluto at the furthest reaches of the sun has always aroused astronomers' curiosity and interests to know more about it.
Revolving is in the closest meaning to this word.
A. deposit   C. milestone
B. rotation   D. obstacle

176. Galileo was a famous Italian astronomer. He used his telescope to make _____ of the moon and the Jupiter, and then made great theories.
Revolving
A. actions   C. selections
B. decisions   D. observations

173. 這名銷售員運用流暢的肢體語言成功地示範廚房用具的操作方式。
Displayed 的意思最接近於這個字。

A. 耕作　　　　C. 宣佈

B. 走私　　　　**D. 示範**

174. 很奇怪的是有些人竟然能夠對於未來即將發生的事做準確的預測。他們甚至宣稱在他們的夢境中親眼目睹那些事件。
Forecasts 的意思最接近於這個字。

A. 探險　　　　**C. 預測**

B. 誘惑　　　　D. 產生

175. 冥王星在距離太陽最遙遠地方的旋轉一向引起天文學者的好奇以及興趣而想作進一步的了解。
Revolving 的意思最接近於這個字。

A. 存款　　　　C. 里程碑

B. 旋轉　　　D. 障礙

176. 伽利略是著名的義大利天文學家。他曾使用望遠鏡對月亮及木星作觀測，因而提出重要的理論。
Watching 的意思最接近於這個字。

A. 行動　　　　C. 挑選

B. 決定　　　　**D. 觀察**

答案　**173.** D　**174.** C　**175.** B　**176.** D

177. Though astronomers and scientists have been trying to make it real for humans to _____ to Mars, the biggest challenge lies in how to get people to and from the planet.

Move is in the closest meaning to this word.

A. express   C. provoke

B. immigrate   D. transplant

178. When asked about the political scandal, the former minister refused to _____ and walked away in haste.

Remark is in the closest meaning to this word.

A. comment   C. idolize

B. expire   D. rehearse

179. Ashley doesn't like to follow trends in her dressing. She has her unique and _____ styles, which makes her distinctive from others.

Creative is in the closest meaning to this word.

A. dedicated   C. righteous

B. original   D. potential

180. Mr. Hamilton was respected for both of his _____ character and boundless enthusiasm in helping others.

Honest is in the closest meaning to this word.

A. mobile   C. upright

B. deceptive   D. controversial

177. 雖然天文學者及科學家一直試圖要把人類移民火星的夢想付諸實現，然而最大的挑戰在於如何讓人們在火星間來回。

Move 的意思最接近於這個字。

A. 表達　　　　　C. 激怒

B. 移民　　　　D. 移植

178. 當被問及政治醜聞的時候，這名前部長拒絕作評論並且倉促離去。

Remark 的意思最接近於這個字。

A. **評論**　　　　C. 崇拜

B. 過期　　　　　D. 排演

179. 艾旭麗在服裝穿著方面不喜歡趕流行。她有她自己獨特且原創的穿衣風格，而就是這一點使得她與眾不同。

Creative 的意思最接近於這個字。

A. 奉獻的　　　　C. 正直的

B. 有創意的　　D. 潛在的

180. 漢彌頓先生以他正直的品格以及助人的高度熱忱受到大家的敬重。

Honest 的意思最接近於這個字。

A. 移動的　　　　C. **正直的**

B. 欺騙的　　　　D. 有爭議的

答案　**177.** B　　**178.** A　　**179.** B　　**180.** C

模擬試題（十六）

✏ Vocabulary in Context

181. The tragic sinking of the British luxury liner ***Titanic*** in 1912 resulted in the heavy casualties of 1,500 deaths out of _____ around 2,500.
Riders is in the closest meaning to this word.
A. documents   C. passengers
B. inhabitants   D. villagers

182. The famous American jazz musician, Louis Armstrong, was not only a popular entertainer but an innovative jazz composer, who greatly _____ and influenced the young music generations.
Encouraged is in the closest meaning to this word.
A. judged   C. inspired
B. delayed   D. intensified

183. Groups of animal lovers held protests to show their disapproval of scientists and labs _____ on animals.
Testing is in the closest meaning to this word.
A. implying   C. testifying
B. opposing   D. experimenting

184. It bothered Barney a lot that his wife had been such ashopaholic that their debts were worsened to a hardly _____ level.

Manageable is in the closest meaning to this word.
A. academic   C. volcanic
B. controllable   D. responsible

181. 在 1912 年，英國豪華郵輪鐵達尼號的不幸沉沒導致大約 2500 名乘客中有 1500 名死亡的重大死傷。
Riders 的意思最接近於這個字。
A. 文件   C. **乘客**
B. 居民   D. 村民

182. 美國著名的爵士音樂家路易斯‧阿姆斯壯，不僅是一名受歡迎的藝人，並 且是一名創新的爵士樂作曲家，他大大地鼓舞以及影響年輕的音樂世代。
Encouraged 的意思最接近於這個字。
A. 批判   C. **鼓舞**
B. 延遲   D. 加強

183. 愛護動物團體為了表明不贊成科學家及實驗室利用動物做實驗而進行抗議。
Testing 的意思最接近於這個字。
A. 暗示   C. 證實
B. 反對   D. **實驗**

184. 巴尼十分困擾於他的妻子是如此糟糕的購物狂以至於他們的債務已經嚴重到無法應付的程度了。
Manageable 的意思最接近於這個字。
A. 學術的   C. 火山的
B. **控制的**   D. 負責的

答案　181. C　182. C　183. D　184. B

185. With the economic recession getting worse, currency inflation has continued and the unemployment rate has _____ to 20%, which in turn triggered social problems.

Towered is in the closest meaning to this word.

A. soared   C. dwelt

B. animated   D. modified

186. The holy water in a small town in France is famed for creating magical curing powers and has yearly attracted lots of pilgrims and tourists all over the world to witness the _____.

Wonder is in the closest meaning to this word.

A. reform   C. portrait

B. miracle   D. civilization

187. The American industrialist, Henry Ford, was a _____ in auto industry, who mass produced cars affordable to average people with the assembly-line technique.

Forerunner is in the closest meaning to this word.

A. victim   C. pioneer

B. critic   D. delinquent

188. Nancy's _____ reaction was to accept Warner's invitation, but after careful consideration, she decided to decline it to avoid misunderstanding.

Beginning is in the closest meaning to this word.

A. initial   C. component

B. negative   D. hypothetical

185. 隨著經濟不景氣日益嚴重，目前通貨膨脹持續不斷，失業率高升至百分之二十，進而引發社會問題。
Towered 的意思最接近於這個字。

A. **高升**　　　　C. 居住
B. 動畫　　　　D. 修改

186. 法國一座小鎮裡的聖水以創造神奇的治療功效而著名，每年吸引許多世界各地的朝聖者及觀光客來見證這一個奇蹟。
Wonder 的意思最接近於這個字。

A. 改革　　　　C. 肖像畫
B. **奇蹟**　　　　D. 文明

187. 美國工業家亨利・福特是汽車工業的先驅，他利用生產線的技術大量製造一般民眾負擔得起的汽車。
Forerunner 的意思最接近於這個字。

A. 受害者　　　　C. **先驅**
B. 評論家　　　　D. 青少年罪犯

188. 南西起初的反應是接受了華納的邀請，但是經過仔細考慮後決定予以婉拒以避免誤會。
Beginning 的意思最接近於這個字。

A. **最初的**　　　　C. 組成的
B. 否定的　　　　D. 假設的

答案　**185.** A　**186.** B　**187.** C　**188.** A

189. The _____ drop in temperatures these days has brought about great damage to crops and the farmed fish.
Sudden is in the closest meaning to this word.
A. charming   C. relevant
B. dramatic   D. overcrowded

190. We all should make every _____ to strengthen our environmental awareness and work out measures to cope with global warming.
Effort is in the closest meaning to this word.
A. endeavor   C. operation
B. impression   D. revenge

191. On hot summer days, children and adults alike find the _____ to eating refreshing ice cream too hard to break down.
Refusal is in the closest meaning to this word.
A. mishap   C. illusion
B. benefit   D. resistance

192. The successful writing of the magic adventures of Harry Potter by J. K. Rowling aroused the _____ of readers all over the world.
Fantasy is in the closest meaning to this word.
A. extinction   C. imagination
B. legislation   D. relaxation

189. 近日氣溫的驟降導致農作物和養殖魚場的重大損傷。
Sudden 的意思最接近於這個字。
A. 迷人的 　　　C. 相關的
B. 戲劇性的 　D. 過度擁擠的

190. 我們都應該努力加強環保意識並且制定對抗全球暖化的對策。
Effort 的意思最接近於這個字。
A. **努力** 　　　C. 操作
B. 印象 　　　　D. 復仇

191. 在炎熱的夏日裡，小孩和大人都認為清涼冰淇淋的誘惑太難以抗拒了。
Refusal 的意思最接近於這個字。
A. 不幸 　　　　C. 幻覺
B. 利益 　　　　D. **抗拒**

192. J. K. 羅琳成功撰寫的哈利波特魔法冒險激發全世界讀者的想像力。
Fantasy 的意思最接近於這個字。
A. 滅絕 　　　　C. **想像**
B. 立法 　　　　D. 放鬆

答案　189. B 　190. A 　191. D 　192. C

模擬試題（十七）

✏ Vocabulary in Context

MP3 017

193. Albert Einstein, the 1921 Nobel Prize winner in physics, made great _____ to the world by his Theory of Relativity, which changed mankind's understanding of science.

Service is in the closest meaning to this word.

A. explanations   C. contributions

B. breakthrough   D. steadiness

194. The entire country is going through an economic _____ and is filled with an atmosphere of uncertainty and anxiety.

Recession is in the closest meaning to this word.

A. famine   C. observance

B. depression   D. assertion

195. Though Mr. Cook's health had notably _____, he remained optimistic and lighthearted for fear that his family might be sad.

Weakened is in the closest meaning to this word.

A. declined   C. kidnapped

B. survived   D. economized

196. The extraordinary new Hollywood actress _____ her position as the most promising future star by her excellent performing skills and high popularity with movie fans.

Secured is in the closest meaning to this word.

A. ruined
C. gossiped
B. portrayed
D. consolidated

193. 艾伯特‧愛因斯坦是 1921 年諾貝爾物理學獎得主，他以改變人類對科學了解的相對論對世界做出極大的貢獻。
Service 的意思最接近於這個字。

A. 解釋
C. **貢獻**
B. 突破
D. 穩定

194. 這整個國家正經歷經濟蕭條的情境，並充塞著不確定和焦慮的氛圍。
Recession 的意思最接近於這個字。

A. 饑荒
C. 遵守
B. **不景氣**
D. 聲稱

195. 雖然庫克先生的健康狀況明顯惡化，但他依然保持樂觀輕鬆的態度，以免他的家人悲傷。
Weakened 的意思最接近於這個字。

A. **衰退**
C. 綁架
B. 倖存
D. 節省

196. 卓越不凡的好萊塢新興女星以她精湛的演技以及超高的人氣鞏固最有前途明日巨星的地位。
Secured 的意思最接近於這個字。

A. 毀壞
C. 閒聊
B. 描繪
D. **鞏固**

答案 **193.** C **194.** B **195.** A **196.** D

197. After going through the serious _____ conditions in the airplane last year, Mrs. Spencer claimed to avoid taking any airplanes because of the strong fear of flights.
Violent is in the closest meaning to this word.
A. flexible   C. obscure
B. elementary   D. turbulent

198. Eco-minded car drivers are encouraged to purchase cars equipped with lower _____ of CO_2 and hybrid engines so as to support global green revolution.
Discharge is in the closest meaning to this word.
A. emissions   C. resources
B. priorities   D. masterpieces

199. According to medical researches, second-hand smoking is closely _____ with lung cancer.
Connected is in the closest meaning to this word.
A. endangered   C. overtaken
B. undergone   D. associated

200. Sean's family and friends shared the joy and honor with him because through constant diligence and _____, his dream of entering an ideal college eventually came true.
Perseverance is in the closest meaning to this word.
A. allergy   C. declaration
B. persistence   D. sentiment

197. 去年在飛機上經歷過嚴重猛烈氣流的狀況後，史班塞太太因為對於飛行強烈的恐懼而聲稱將避免搭乘飛機。
Violent 的意思最接近於這個字。
A. 有彈性的　　　C. 不清楚的
B. 基礎的　　　　**D. 猛烈的**

198. 具有環保觀念的駕駛被鼓勵去購買配備有二氧化碳低排放量以及油電混合引擎的汽車以支持地球的綠色革命。
Discharge 的意思最接近於這個字。
A. **排放**　　　C. 資源
B. 優先　　　　D. 傑作

199. 根據醫學研究，二手煙與肺癌有密切的關係。
Connected 的意思最接近於這個字。
A. 危及　　　　C. 趕上
B. 經歷　　　　**D. 聯想**

200. 尚恩的家人和朋友與他共享喜悅和榮耀，因為經由持續不斷的努力和堅持，他終於實現了進入理想大學的夢想。
Perseverance 的意思最接近於這個字。
A. 過敏　　　　C. 宣佈
B. **堅持**　　　D. 感情

 答案 **197.** D　**198.** A　**199.** D　**200.** B

201. After five years of hard-working, Eddie was _____ promoted to the managerial position, and all of his colleagues agreed that he deserved the advancement.
Finally is in the closest meaning to this word.
A. largely   C. eventually
B. systematically   D. simultaneously

202. It is taken for granted that you will be seriously punished if you violate the traffic _____ by driving in the wrong direction.
Rules is in the closest meaning to this word.
A. donations   C. solutions
B. regulations   D. quotations

203. With lots of photos and signatures of movie stars hung on the wall, the famous restaurant was _____ as a dining place frequented by celebrities and movie stars.
Characterized is in the closest meaning to this word.
A. featured   C. prohibited
B. refused   D. allocated

204. Myron was _____ as the leader of the project team and was fully dedicated to the realization of his new ideas.
Appointed is in the closest meaning to this word.
A. analyzed   C. designated
B. ornamented   D. reproached

201. 經過五年的努力之後，艾迪終於被擢升到經理的職位，他所有的同事都一致認為這份升遷是他應得的。
Finally 的意思最接近於這個字。
A. 主要地　　　C. **最終地**
B. 系統地　　　D. 同時地

202. 你因逆向行駛違反交通規則而被嚴厲處罰是件理所當然的事。
Rules 的意思最接近於這個字。
A. 捐贈　　　C. 解決方案
B. **規則**　　　D. 引語

203. 這家著名的餐廳牆上掛著許多電影明星的照片和簽名，它最大的特色在於它是名流和電影明星經常光顧的用餐地點。
Characterized 的意思最接近於這個字。
A. **特色**　　　C. 禁止
B. 拒絕　　　D. 分配

204. 麥倫被指派去擔任專案小組的領導人並努力執行他的新點子。
Appointed 的意思最接近於這個字。
A. 分析　　　C. **指派**
B. 裝飾　　　D. 責備

答案　**201.** C　**202.** B　**203.** A　**204.** C

18 UNIT

模擬試題（十八）

✏ Vocabulary in Context

205. The doctor advised the _____ to quit smoking and drinking for the sake of his health.
Sufferer is in the closest meaning to this word.
A. patient
C. consultant
B. surgeon
D. archaeologist

206. After one whole week's work, Gavin made himself _____ and enjoyed the pleasant Friday night by watching TV and eating snacks on the sofa.
Relaxed is in the closest meaning to this word.
A. savage
C. comfortable
B. pious
D. extravagant

207. Mr. Emerson consulted a _____ and was prescribed some medicine for his high blood pressure.
Doctor is in the closest meaning to this word.
A. executive
C. physician
B. trader
D. dictator

208. Leo's interpersonal relationships _____ significantly after he became friendly and active in socializing with others.
Bettered is in the closest meaning to this word.
A. summoned
C. postponed
B. improved
D. grieved

205. 醫生忠告病患為了健康著想，他應該要戒菸以及戒酒。
Sufferer 的意思最接近於這個字。
A. **病患**　　　C. 顧問
B. 外科醫生　　D. 考古學家

206. 經過一整個禮拜辛苦的工作，蓋文坐在沙發上看電視以及吃點心，很舒適地享受愉快的周五夜晚。
Relaxed 的意思最接近於這個字。
A. 野蠻的　　　C. **舒服的**
B. 虔誠的　　　D. 浪費的

207. 愛默生先生看內科醫生，醫生為他開了治療高血壓的處方。
Doctor 的意思最接近於這個字。
A. 執行長　　　C. **內科醫生**
B. 貿易商　　　D. 獨裁者

208. 李奧在變得友善以及主動地與別人來往後，他的人際關係有極大的改善。
Bettered 的意思最接近於這個字。
A. 召喚　　　　C. 延遲
B. **改善**　　　D. 哀傷

答案　**205.** A　**206.** C　**207.** C　**208.** B

209. Penicillin, a substance used as a drug to treat or prevent bacteria-caused infections, is undoubtedly the greatest _____ discovery of the 20th century.

Therapeutic is in the closest meaning to this word.

A. medical   C. commercial

B. restless   D. protective

210. The Oscar-winning director Ang Lee adopted advanced movie _____ in his latest film about American soldiers returning home from Iraq, Billy Lynn.

Skills is in the closest meaning to this word.

A. fiction   C. penetration

B. regime   D. technology

211. Deeply _____ by his parents' unhappy marriage and divorce, Derrick was afraid to make any commitment and stayed single till he met Nora.

Affected is in the closest meaning to this word.

A. moved   C. influenced

B. tolerated   D. extinguished

212. To Todd, it was such a great _____ to have the chance to interview the contemporary Japanese master of animation.

Honor is in the closest meaning to this word.

A. utility   C. sequence

B. privilege   D. modesty

209. 盤尼西林是一種用來治療或預防細菌感染的藥物，它無疑地是二十世紀最偉大的醫學發現。

Therapeutic 的意思最接近於這個字。

A. **醫學的**　　　　C. 廣告的

B. 焦躁不安的　　D. 保護的

210. 奧斯卡得獎導演李安在他最新描述有關於美國士兵從伊拉克返鄉的電影《比利‧林恩》中採用了先進的電影拍攝技術。

Skills 的意思最接近於這個字。

A. 杜撰小說　　　C. 貫穿

B. 政權　　　　　D. **技術**

211. 深受父母親不愉快的婚姻以及離婚的影響，戴瑞克在遇見諾拉之前一直畏懼於做出承諾並且保持單身。

Affected 的意思最接近於這個字。

A. 感動　　　　　C. **影響**

B. 忍受　　　　　D. 熄滅

212. 對陶德來說，能夠有機會去訪問當代日本動畫大師是一項極大的殊榮。

Honor 的意思最接近於這個字。

A. 效用　　　　　C. 順序

B. **殊榮**　　　　D. 謙虛

答案　**209.** A　**210.** D　**211.** C　**212.** B

213. The witness positively _____ the young suspect as the person who robbed the old lady of her bag the other night.

Distinguished is in the closest meaning to this word.

A. identified   C. modified

B. recruited   D. assaulted

214. Modern people are encouraged to take regular physical check-ups, as the earlier certain illnesses are _____, the sooner they can be treated and cured.

Analyzed is in the closest meaning to this word.

A. speculated   C. compressed

B. ascended   D. diagnosed

215. In the era of _____, what everyone should do is to develop creativity and originality so as to remain competitive.

Creation is in the closest meaning to this word.

A. dignity   C. warranty

B. souvenir   D. innovation

216. For quite a long time, overdevelopment in industry has had a strong _____ on earth, which illustrates the importance of strengthening common people's environmental awareness.

Influence is in the closest meaning to this word.

A. mercy   C. impact

B. switch   D. description

213. 目擊證人很有把握地指認這名年輕嫌疑犯是前一晚搶奪老婦人皮包的搶匪。

Distinguished 的意思最接近於這個字。

A. **辨認**　　　C. 改良

B. 招募　　　　D. 突襲

214. 現代人被鼓勵要定期做健康檢查，因為特定疾病的病情越早被診斷出來就可以越快接受治療並痊癒。

Analyzed 的意思最接近於這個字。

A. 推測　　　　C. 壓縮

B. 升高　　　　D. **診斷**

215. 在這個創新的時代中，人人所應該要做的是發展創意和獨創性以保持競爭力。

Creation 的意思最接近於這個字。

A. 尊嚴　　　　C. 擔保

B. 紀念品　　　D. **創新**

216. 長時間以來，工業的過度發展對於地球造成嚴重的衝擊，因此突顯出加強一般民眾環保意識的重要。

Influence 的意思最接近於這個字。

A. 慈悲　　　　C. **衝擊**

B. 轉換　　　　D. 描述

答案　**213.** A　**214.** D　**215.** D　**216.** C

模擬試題（十九）

Vocabulary in Context

MP3 019

217. The firefighters tried their best to come to the _____ of the old couple from the burning apartment, but in vain.
Saving is in the closest meaning to this word.
A. rescue   C. fulfillment
B. brood   D. optimism

218. In high school days, Adam used to boast about becoming a manager and making a lot of money. _____, he works only as a janitor in a mall now.
Sarcastically is in the closest meaning to this word.
A. Personally   C. Generously
B. Temporarily   D. Ironically

219. In _____, you could take all the work assigned to you. However, in practice, is it possible for you to finish it all by yourself?
Supposition is in the closest meaning to this word.
A. fact   C. analysis
B. theory   D. melody

220. After being _____ from the prison for only a few months, the ex-convict was put in jail again for lacking money and committing crimes again.
Freed is in the closest meaning to this word.
A. traced   C. released
B. amplified   D. deceived

217. 消防人員盡最大的力量試圖從燃燒的公寓中將老夫婦救出，但卻徒勞無功。

Saving 的意思最接近於這個字。

A. **拯救**　　　C. 實現

B. 沉思　　　　D. 樂觀

218. 高中時期，亞當時常自誇要成為公司經理並且賺大錢。諷刺的是，現在他只是一名大賣場裡的清潔人員。

Sarcastically 的意思最接近於這個字。

A. 個人地　　　C. 慷慨地

B. 暫時地　　　D. **諷刺地**

219. 理論上來說，你可以接受所有指派給你的工作。但是，實際上，你有辦法獨自完成所有的工作嗎？。

Supposition 的意思最接近於這個字。

A. 事實　　　　C. 分析

B. **理論**　　　D. 旋律

220. 這名前科犯出獄不過幾個月，因缺錢花用而犯案，於是又再度入獄了。

Freed 的意思最接近於這個字。

A. 跟蹤　　　　C. **釋放**

B. 放大　　　　D. 欺騙

答案 **217.** A　**218.** D　**219.** B　**220.** C

221. The _____ damage of the disaster was so large that there was no way of making any actual estimation.
Overall is in the closest meaning to this word.
A. high-class   C. close-ranged
B. time-proven   D. full-scale

222. Among all the public _____ means in the city, the MRT is the most convenient and the most popular one.
Commuting is in the closest meaning to this word.
A. media   C. coordination
B. transportation   D. opposition

223. The late philanthropist was kind-hearted and generous, whose charity deeds were meaningful and _____.
Countless is in the closest meaning to this word.
A. uncountable   C. numerical
B. climatic   D. redundant

224. When it comes to _____, the Wright brothers were the greatest and the earliest pioneers.
Flight is in the closest meaning to this word.
A. diplomacy   C. volcano
B. reforestation   D. aviation

221. 這次災難整體的損害是如此地嚴重以致於無法做確切的評估。
Overall 的意思最接近於這個字。
A. 高級的 　　　 C. 近距離的
B. 不變的 　　　 **D. 全面的**

222. 所有都市裡的大眾運輸工具中，捷運是最方便，同時也是最受歡迎的。
Commuting 的意思最接近於這個字。
A. 媒體 　　　 C. 協調
B. 交通運輸 　 D. 反對

223. 這名已故的慈善家既仁慈又慷慨，他的善行深具意義而且難以計數。
Countless 的意思最接近於這個字。
A. 無法計算的 　 C. 數字的
B. 氣候的 　　　 D. 多餘的

224. 談到飛行，萊特兄弟是最偉大而且是最早期的先驅。
Flight 的意思最接近於這個字。
A. 外交 　　　 C. 火山
B. 重新造林 　　 **D. 飛行**

答案 **221.** D **222.** B **223.** A **224.** D

225. Detesting being bossed around, Terry decided to _____ from the low-ranked position and started his own company.
Quit is in the closest meaning to this word.
A. deliver   C. originate
B. resign   D. anticipate

226. The enterprise has set up plans to _____ its operations only on merchandise of easy sale so as to maximize profits.
Focus is in the closest meaning to this word.
A. oppress   C. concentrate
B. fascinate   D. restrain

227. In the airport, hundreds of baseball fans welcomed the _____ heroes, who had just won the world championship.
Triumphant is in the closest meaning to this word.
A. prevalent   C. justifiable
B. conquering   D. pessimistic

228. Bruce felt frustrated and stressed when the professor informed him of the fact that his doctoral dissertation needed considerable _____.
Alteration is in the closest meaning to this word.
A. collection   C. vaccination
B. reproduction   D. modification

225. 泰瑞厭惡被指使，於是決定辭去低階的工作而去開創自己的公司。
Quit 的意思最接近於這個字。

A. 傳遞　　　　C. 起源於

B. **辭職**　　　　D. 預期

226. 這家公司訂定計畫集中銷售容易販賣的商品以增加到最大的利潤。
Focus 的意思最接近於這個字。

A. 壓迫　　　　**C. 專注於**

B. 著迷　　　　D. 節制

227. 在機場裡，上百名棒球球迷歡迎凱旋而歸的英雄，他們剛剛獲得世界冠軍。
Triumphant 的意思最接近於這個字。

A. 流行的　　　C. 有道理的

B. **戰勝的**　　　D. 悲觀的

228. 當教授通知他的博士論文需要做大篇幅修改時，布魯斯感受到極大的挫折與壓力。
Alteration 的意思最接近於這個字。

A. 收集　　　　C. 接種疫苗

B. 複製　　　　**D. 修改**

答案　**225.** B　**226.** C　**227.** B　**228.** D

20 UNIT 模擬試題（二十）

✏ Vocabulary in Context   MP3 020

229. In many _____ countries, lovers celebrate Valentine's Day on February 14. They give each other cards and presents like flowers and chocolate. At night, they enjoy a romantic candlelight dinner together.
Occidental is in the closest meaning to this word.
A. western   C. redundant
B. spatial   D. eligible

230. The CEO read the files and discussed about the investment projects with his consultants while taking a _____ flight.
Continent-crossing is in the closest meaning to this word.
A. courteous   C. multicultural
B. honorary   D. transcontinental

231. The _____ city in Turkey has been famous and popular for its structural and historical mystery, which attracts tourists all over the world for sightseeing.
Subterranean is in the closest meaning to this word.
A. compatible   C. underground
B. liberal   D. circular

232. _____ as Mr. Ford was, his real talent and interest lay in music.

Enterpriser is in the closest meaning to this word.
A. Juvenile
B. Industrialist
C. Folklore
D. Witness

229. 在許多西方國家裡，情侶在二月十四日慶祝情人節。他們彼此互送卡片及像花以及巧克力的禮物。在夜晚，他們共享浪漫的燭光晚餐。

Occidental 的意思最接近於這個字。

A. **西方的**
B. 空間的
C. 多餘的
D. 合格的

230. 在搭乘橫貫大陸的飛行途中，這名總裁閱讀資料並且和顧問討論投資計畫。

Continent-crossing 的意思最接近於這個字。

A. 有禮貌的
B. 名譽的
C. 多元文化的
D. **橫貫大陸的**

231. 土耳其地下城一向以它結構及歷史的神祕受到注目以及歡迎，而就是這項特點吸引世界各地的觀光客前往一遊。

Subterranean 的意思最接近於這個字。

A. 相容的
B. 自由的
C. **地下的**
D. 循環的

232. 雖然福特先生是一名工業家，他真正的天分和興趣是在於音樂。

Enterpriser 的意思最接近於這個字。

A. 青少年
B. **工業家**
C. 民俗
D. 目擊者

答案 **229.** A　**230.** D　**231.** C　**232.** B

233. It was disappointing that the whole speech didn't get to the point. The speaker should have _____ himself strictly to the subject.
Restricted is in the closest meaning to this word.
A. confined   C. fostered
B. echoed   D. trespassed

234. The _____ of John F. Kennedy was one of the world's most shocking moments, and the whole nation mourned over the death of the promising young president, who was expected to accomplish great deeds.
Murder is in the closest meaning to this word.
A. efficiency   C. introspection
B. genius   D. assassination

235. Without doubt, the successful _____ and marketing strategies contributed to not only the popularity of Korean culture but the big sales of Korean products.
Propaganda is in the closest meaning to this word.
A. publicity   C. fragment
B. classification   D. misconduct

236. People living in democracy are lucky to enjoy _____ from want and fear, and above all, freedom of speech.
Liberty is in the closest meaning to this word.
A. morality   C. freedom
B. transmission   D. evolution

233. 令人失望的是整場演講都離題了。演講者應該嚴謹地切合主題做演說。

Restricted 的意思最接近於這個字。

A. **限制**　　　　C. 培養

B. 回聲　　　　D. 擅自進入

234. 約翰‧甘迺迪總統遇刺是令世人感到最震驚的時刻之一，全國民眾哀悼這位原先被預期將有偉大成就、前途被看好的年輕總統之死。

Murder 的意思最接近於這個字。

A. 效率　　　　C. 反省

B. 天份　　　　D. **暗殺**

235. 無疑地，成功的宣傳和行銷策略不僅促成韓國文化的廣受歡迎並且使得韓國商品大賣。

Propaganda 的意思最接近於這個字。

A. **宣傳**　　　　C. 片段

B. 分類　　　　D. 不良行為

236. 民主政治下的人們很幸運地享受不虞匱乏以及免於恐懼的自由，尤其是享有言論自由。

Liberty 的意思最接近於這個字。

A. 道德　　　　C. **自由**

B. 傳送　　　　D. 演化

答案　**233.** A　**234.** D　**235.** A　**236.** C

237. Leonardo da Vinci was a remarkable genius, who _____ in painting, sculpture, architecture, and inventing.
Surpassed is in the closest meaning to this word.
A. hosted   C. substituted
B. excelled   D. undermined

238. To _____ goals in life, Carl did his utmost to enrich knowledge on one hand and broaden his life experiences on the other.
Accomplish is in the closest meaning to this word.
A. isolate   C. achieve
B. reconcile   D. oppress

239. After Max was _____ the Best-Employee of the Year, he worked even harder and eventually got promoted as the store manager.
Given is in the closest meaning to this word.
A. awarded   C. violated
B. represented   D. gratified

240. The distinguished alumnus generously left an _____ of three million dollars to the university to show his gratitude and support.
Contribution is in the closest meaning to this word.
A. population   C. unemployment
B. impression   D. endowment

237. 李奧納多・達文西是一名精通於繪畫、雕刻、建築，以及發明的曠世奇才。

Surpassed 的意思最接近於這個字。

A. 主持　　　　C. 替代

B. 優於　　　D. 破壞

238. 為了達成人生的目標，卡爾一方面盡力充實知識，另一方面則拓展人生經驗。

Accomplish 的意思最接近於這個字。

A. 孤立　　　　**C. 達成**

B. 和解　　　　D. 壓迫

239. 麥克斯獲頒年度最佳員工獎之後更加努力地工作，最終獲升遷為商店經理。

Given 的意思最接近於這個字。

A. 頒發　　　C. 違反

B. 代表　　　　D. 感激

240. 這位傑出校友很慷慨地捐贈三百萬元給大學以表示他的感激和支持。

Contribution 的意思最接近於這個字。

A. 人口　　　　C. 失業

B. 印象　　　　**D. 捐贈**

答案　**237.** B　**238.** C　**239.** A　**240.** D

模擬試題（二十一）

✎ Vocabulary in Context

241. Huge heavy motorcycles in Taiwan not only cause a lot of air _____ but disturb people in quiet neighborhoods, which arouses serious complaints from the general public.
Contamination is in the closest meaning to this word.
A. foundation
C. pollution
B. control
D. survey

242. _____ speaking, in order to look young and perfect, nowadays, more and more people turn to plastic surgery, though the cost may be amazingly high.
Comparatively is in the closest meaning to this word.
A. Steadily
C. Inconveniently
B. Relatively
D. Medically

243. Shouldering _____ responsibility to support the family, Roy couldn't but take several part-time jobs besides his regular work.
Huge is in the closest meaning to this word.
A. enormous
C. relevant
B. industrious
D. miraculous

244. The stressful work and the chronic diseases _____ to Mr. Dewey's serious insomnia at night.
Caused is in the closest meaning to this word.
A. authorized
C. subscribed
B. installed
D. contributed

241. 台灣的大型重型機車不僅製造大量的空氣汙染，同時也干擾到寧靜住家的住戶們，因此引發一般大眾嚴重的抱怨。
Contamination 的意思最接近於這個字。
   A. 基礎　　　　　　C. **污染**
   B. 管制　　　　　　D. 調查

242. 相對而言，雖然花費可能高的驚人，為了要看起來年輕完美，現在越來越多人選擇做整容手術。
Comparatively 的意思最接近於這個字。
   A. 穩定地　　　　　C. 不方便地
   B. **相對地**　　　　D. 醫療上地

243. 羅伊肩負著養家的重大責任，不得不在正規工作之外兼數份差。
Huge 的意思最接近於這個字。
   A. **巨大的**　　　　C. 相關的
   B. 勤勉的　　　　　D. 奇蹟的

244. 極具壓力的工作以及慢性疾病導致杜威先生夜晚嚴重的失眠。
Caused 的意思最接近於這個字。
   A. 授權　　　　　　C. 訂閱
   B. 安裝　　　　　　D. **促成**

答案　**241.** C　**242.** B　**243.** A　**244.** D

245. The _____ of the residents were strongly against the construction of a new chemical plant around their neighborhood and planned to stage a protest.
Most is in the closest meaning to this word.
A. grade　　　　　C. distribution
B. region　　　　　D. majority

246. With the health awareness prevailing, _____ foods, vegetables and fruits have been in high demand these days.
Natural is in the closest meaning to this word.
A. recycling　　　C. democratic
B. organic　　　　D. alternative

247. As a whole, it's difficult to strike a balance between promoting the global economic growth and lessening the _____ impact of pollution on humans.
Surroundings is in the closest meaning to this word.
A. considerate　　C. environmental
B. identical　　　　D. violent

248. The best solution to the issue is to _____ the old prejudice and bad feelings toward each other and cooperate again.
Abandon is in the closest meaning to this word.
A. discard　　　　C. witness
B. complicate　　D. participate

245. 大多數的居民強烈反對在他們的住家附近建造一座新的化工工廠，並且計畫發動抗議活動。

Most 的意思最接近於這個字。

A. 等級　　　　　C. 分配

B. 區域　　　　　**D. 大多數**

246. 隨著健康意識的流行，近日有機食物、蔬菜，以及水果的需求量大增。

Natural 的意思最接近於這個字。

A. 回收的　　　　C. 民主的

B. 有機的　　　D. 替代的

247. 整體而言，要尋求促進全球經濟成長以及減緩環境污染對於人類的衝擊兩者之間的平衡是困難的。

Surrounding 的意思最接近於這個字。

A. 體貼的　　　　**C. 環境的**

B. 相同的　　　　D. 暴力的

248. 這個問題最佳的解決方法是拋棄原舊有的偏見以及彼此不良的印象而再度齊心合作。

Abandon 的意思最接近於這個字。

A. **拋棄**　　　　C. 目睹

B. 使複雜　　　　D. 參加

 答案 **245.** D　**246.** B　**247.** C　**248.** A

Part 1 同義字模擬試題

Part 2 填空題模擬試題

Part 3 聽、讀整合能力強化

249. After retirement from the public office, Mr. Costner worked in a private corporation as a _____ on business affairs.

Adviser is in the closest meaning to this word.

A. hitchhiker   C. consultant

B. pharmacist   D. technician

250. Undoubtedly, the rapid progress in the development and outcome of _____ intelligence will take the mankind to a brand-new era.

Man-made is in the closest meaning to this word.

A. visual   C. revolutionary

B. flexible   D. artificial

251. The police intensively _____ possible links between the suspect and the case of suicide, in which telecommunications fraud was allegedly to have cost the victim huge amounts of his pension.

Inspected is in the closest meaning to this word.

A. deterred   C. investigated

B. measured   D. sentenced

252. The researcher _____ collected and analyzed the samples to prove the hypotheses he suggested.

Orderly is in the closest meaning to this word.

A. commercially   C. negatively

B. systematically   D. prehistorically

249. 從公職退休後，科斯納先生在私人公司擔任商業顧問。
Adviser 的意思最接近於這個字。
A. 搭便車者　　C. **顧問**
B. 藥劑師　　　D. 技術人員

250. 無疑地，人工智慧發展及結果的快速進步將會把人類帶入一個全新的紀元。
Man-made 的意思最接近於這個字。
A. 視覺的　　　C. 革命的
B. 彈性的　　　D. **人工的**

251. 警方密切地調查這名嫌疑犯和一樁自殺案件可能存在的關聯性，據說電信詐騙使得受害者損失大筆的退休金。
Inspected 的意思最接近於這個字。
A. 阻止　　　C. **調查**
B. 測量　　　D. 宣判

252. 這名研究人員有系統地收集分析樣本以證實他提出的假設。
Orderly 的意思最接近於這個字。
A. 商業地　　　C. 消極地
B. **有系統地**　D. 史前地

答案　**249.** C　**250.** D　**251.** C　**252.** B

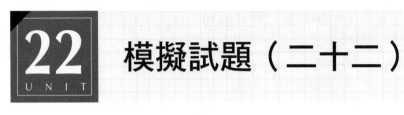

22 模擬試題（二十二）

U N I T

✏️ Vocabulary in Context

253. The Internet brings us a lot of access and conveniences; with only a click of the mouse, we can make collection and _____ of information easily.
Transmission is in the closest meaning to this word.
A. adversity   C. immunity
B. transit   D. reinforcement

254. Simon was experienced and well-trained in his field and was chosen as an agent to _____ the company.
Delegate is in the closest meaning to this word.
A. harass   C. represent
B. issue   D. anticipate

255. It was the British naturalist Charles Darwin who established the theory that species _____ through the process of natural selection over long ages.
Develop is in the closest meaning to this word.
A. evolve   C. discriminate
B. thrive   D. navigate

256. The Nasca Lines in Peru consist of several thousands of geometric _____ and hundreds of distinct animal shapes and have been a great mystery for all time.
Designs is in the closest meaning to this word.
A. effects   C. patterns
B. welfare   D. microscope

253. 網際網路為我們帶來許多捷徑以及便利；點一下滑鼠，我們就可以輕鬆地收集以及傳送資訊。

Transmission 的意思最接近於這個字。

A. 逆境　　　　　C. 免疫

B. **傳送**　　　　D. 加強

254. 賽門在他的領域經驗豐富並且訓練有素，因此被選為代表公司的負責人。

Delegate 的意思最接近於這個字。

A. 騷擾　　　　　C. **代表**

B. 發行　　　　　D. 預期

255. 英國博物學家查爾斯・達爾文提出理論認為物種是經由長時間物競天擇的過程演變而成的。

Developed 的意思最接近於這個字。

A. **演化**　　　　C. 歧視

B. 興盛　　　　　D. 航行

256. 祕魯的納斯卡線是由數千條幾何圖案及上百個明顯的動物形狀圖案所組成的，長久以來一直是個謎。

Designs 的意思最接近於這個字。

A. 效果　　　　　C. **圖案**

B. 福利　　　　　D. 顯微鏡

答案　**253.** B　**254.** C　**255.** A　**256.** C

257. It's a pity that Michael Jackson, who has been an _____ to his pop music fans, died young; otherwise, they could enjoy more of his wonderful works and performances.
Encouragement is in the closest meaning to this word.
A. alienation   C. oppression
B. element   D. inspiration

258. Though it took Emma several months to _____ to the new working environment, she made it and did a great job.
Adjust is in the closest meaning to this word.
A. adapt   C. diminish
B. resist   D. compliment

259. As the books in the library are _____ according to their subjects, it's easy to find the books you want.
Categorized is in the closest meaning to this word.
A. reigned   C. classified
B. nominated   D. innovated

260. The factory decided to modernize the _____ to meet the increasing demand of both domestic and foreign orders.
Equipment is in the closest meaning to this word.
A. utensils   C. apparatus
B. variation   D. ecosystem

257. 令人惋惜的一件事是對於流行樂迷來說一直是鼓舞力量的麥可・傑克遜英年早逝；否則他們可以享受更多他精彩的作品以及表演。
Encouragement 的意思最接近於這個字。
A. 疏離　　　　C. 壓迫
B. 元素　　　　**D. 鼓舞**

258. 雖然艾瑪花了好幾個月的時間去適應新的工作環境，然而她成功了並且表現優異。
Adjust 的意思最接近於這個字。
A. 適應　　　C. 削減
B. 抗拒　　　　D. 稱讚

259. 由於圖書館裡的書籍是按照主題分類的，你很容易就可以找到你所要的書籍。
Categorized 的意思最接近於這個字。
A. 統治　　　　**C. 分類**
B. 提名　　　　D. 革新

260. 這座工廠決定將設備現代化以符合國內外訂貨量逐漸增加的需求。
Equipment 的意思最接近於這個字。
A. 餐具　　　　**C. 設備**
B. 變化　　　　D. 生態系統

答案　**257.** D　**258.** A　**259.** C　**260.** C

261. Miss Lopez is a popular foreign _____ in Spanish. She not only makes Spanish interesting and easy to learn but also shows great patience and passion to her students.
Teacher is in the closest meaning to this word.
A. curator
C. ballerina
B. instructor
D. inhabitant

262. _____ innovations in industry have been significant in improving products and raising humans' living standards.
Technological is in the closest meaning to this word.
A. Random
C. Glamorous
B. Abnormal
D. Technical

263. The experience of being a part-time design _____ at night helped Gina a lot in getting official full-time employment as a formal designer after her college graduation.
Helper is in the closest meaning to this word.
A. diplomat
C. pessimist
B. assistant
D. disturber

264. After election, Mr. Major was finally formally _____ into the office of mayor and started fulfilling his campaign promises.
Inaugurated is in the closest meaning to this word.
A. inducted
C. comprehended
B. retrieved
D. disciplined

261. 羅培茲小姐是一位很受歡迎的西班牙語教師。她不僅使得西班牙語的學習變得有趣輕鬆，並且對學生展現極大的耐心及熱情。
Teacher 的意思最接近於這個字。
A. 館長　　　　　C. 女芭蕾舞者
B. **教師**　　　　D. 居民

262. 工業的技術革新在改善產品品質及提升人類生活水準方面具有重大的意義。
Technological 的意思最接近於這個字。
A. 隨機的　　　　C. 富有魅力的
B. 反常的　　　　D. **技術的**

263. 夜間擔任兼差設計助理的經驗在吉娜大學畢業後取得擔任全職的正式設計師工作上有極大的幫助。
Helper 的意思最接近於這個字。
A. 外交官　　　　C. 悲觀者
B. **助理**　　　　D. 干擾者

264. 選舉過後，梅傑先生終於正式就任市長的職位，並且開始實踐他的競選承諾。
Inaugurated 的意思最接近於這個字。
A. **就任**　　　　C. 理解
B. 收回　　　　　D. 訓練

答案　261. B　262. D　263. B　264. A

23 模擬試題（二十三）

UNIT

✎ Vocabulary in Context

MP3 023

265. Though the kidnapper _____ to kill the hostage if he didn't get the ransom, with his location spotted, he was soon nailed and the hostage was saved.
Menaced is in the closest meaning to this word.
A. affected   C. threatened
B. consulted   D. monitored

266. After Marvin was appointed to _____ the international conference, he devoted himself fully to accomplishing the work.
Arrange is in the closest meaning to this word.
A. organize   C. select
B. arise   D. perceive

267. With the Internet _____ to us, we can achieve a lot of things; in the meantime, we should be careful not to get addicted or fall victim to net frauds.
Available is in the closest meaning to this word.
A. traditional   C. radiant
B. enormous   D. accessible

268. The Japanese mountaineer Junko Tabei was the first woman to conquer Mount Everest in 1975. To her, it was the willpower, together with technique and capability, that helped her _____ the impossible task.

Achieve is in the closest meaning to this word.
A. foretell
C. manufacture
B. accomplish
D. trigger

265. 雖然綁匪威脅假使拿不到贖金要殺害人質，但是隨著所在處曝光，他很快地被逮捕，人質因而獲救。
Menaced 的意思最接近於這個字。
A. 影響
C. **威脅**
B. 諮詢
D. 監督

266. 馬文被指派籌劃國際會議之後，他全心投入於把工作做好。
Arrange 的意思最接近於這個字。
A. **籌備**
C. 選擇
B. 發生
D. 察覺

267. 有著網際網路供我們便捷地利用，我們可以成就許多事情；在這同時，我們應該要謹慎，不要網路成癮，或是成為網路詐欺的受害者。
Available 的意思最接近於這個字。
A. 傳統的
C. 容光煥發的
B. 巨大的
D. **可使用的**

268. 日籍登山家，田部井淳子，在 1975 年成為第一位征服聖母峰的女性。對她而言，意志力，連同技術和能力，幫助她完成不可能的任務。
Achieve 的意思最接近於這個字。
A. 預告
C. 製造
B. **完成**
D. 觸發

答案 265. C   266. A   267. D   268. B

Part 1 同義字模擬試題

Part 2 填空題模擬試題

Part 3 聽、讀整合能力強化

269. _____ within the Bermuda Islands, the Bermuda Triangle is an area abounded by Florida, Bermuda, and Puerto Rico, where ships and planes would vanish mysteriously.

Situated is in the closest meaning to this word.

A. Located
C. Deceived

B. Transformed
D. Overestimated

270. Robots have been useful in the industry and the household. Now in Japan, they also _____ service in the medical field, such as nursing, lifting andtransporting patients, recording and monitoring patients' medical condition.

Provide is in the closest meaning to this word.

A. abolish
C. offer

B. undergo
D. plagiarise

271. While scientists _____ nanotechnology to benefit mankind in many fields, both the manipulation and the side-effects of the technology cannot be overemphasized.

Use is in the closest meaning to this word.

A. scan
C. circulate

B. overwhelm
D. utilize

272. To cope with the problems of global warming, the public are _____ to recycle and reuse everything, take the mass transportation, and use the electricity economically.

Inspired is in the closest meaning to this word.

A. browsed
C. encouraged

B. legislated
D. rehabilitated

269. 百慕達三角位於百慕達群島中，它是由佛羅里達、百慕達，和波多黎各所環繞而成的區域，在此處船隻和飛機會神秘地消失。
Situated 的意思最接近於這個字。
A. **位於**　　　　C. 欺騙
B. 轉變　　　　D. 高估

270. 機器人一向實用於工業以及家庭。現今在日本，它們也提供醫療方面的服務，譬如照料、搬移以及護送病患，紀錄並且監督病患的醫療狀況。
Provide 的意思最接近於這個字。
A. 廢除　　　　C. **提供**
B. 經歷　　　　D. 剽竊

271. 科學家利用奈米科技於許多領域以嘉惠人類，然而這項技術的操作以及副作用也應該予以高度地重視。
Use 的意思最接近於這個字。
A. 掃描　　　　C. 循環
B. 壓倒　　　　D. **利用**

272. 為了要對抗全球暖化的問題，大眾被鼓勵要回收並再利用所有的東西，搭乘大眾運輸系統，以及節約用電。
Inspired 的意思最接近於這個字。
A. 瀏覽　　　　C. **鼓勵**
B. 立法　　　　D. 康復

答案 **269.** A　**270.** C　**271.** D　**272.** C

273. Donna and Scott were in serious _____ over cloning. The former felt that safe cloning to prolong humans' life was OK, while the later was against the idea of playing God. ***Argument*** is in the closest meaning to this word.

A. disagreement   C. revision

B. tourism   D. eruption

274. Knowing the _____ of winning the first prize in the international competition, the coach and all the teammates exclaimed with great joy. ***Outcome*** is in the closest meaning to this word.

A. immunity   C. principle

B. result   D. circumstance

275. Strange and scary dreams often bother people a lot. However, according to researchers, dreams _____ only responses to events in dreamers' personal life and can help us understand ourselves more. ***Mirror*** is in the closest meaning to this word.

A. execute   C. alleviate

B. reflect   D. contaminate

276. William's driving license was _____ for drunk driving, which he later bitterly regretted having done. ***Stopped*** is in the closest meaning to this word.

A. analyzed   C. facilitated

B. congested   D. suspended

273. 唐娜和史考特對於複製的看法嚴重分歧。前者認為，使用安全的複製方法以延長人類壽命是可行的，然而，後者反對這個扮演上帝的想法。

Argument 的意思最接近於這個字。

A. **意見分歧**　　C. 校訂

B. 觀光業　　　　D. 爆發

274. 得知在國際競賽中獲得第一名的結果，教練和所有的隊員高興地歡呼。

Outcome 的意思最接近於這個字。

A. 免疫　　　　C. 原則

B. **結果**　　　　D. 情境

275. 奇怪且嚇人的夢境經常令大眾感到十分困擾。然而，根據研究學者的說法，夢境只是反映出做夢者日常生活事件的反應，並且可以幫助我們多了解自己。

Mirror 的意思最接近於這個字。

A. 執行　　　　C. 減緩

B. **反映**　　　　D. 污染

276. 威廉的駕照因酒駕被暫時中止，他事後對於自己的行為感到相當後悔。

Stopped 的意思最接近於這個字。

A. 分析　　　　C. 使便利

B. 擁塞　　　　D. **暫時中止**

答案　**273.** A　**274.** B　**275.** B　**276.** D

24 UNIT

模擬試題（二十四）

✏ Vocabulary in Context

277. Arthur was hopelessly _____ to sports betting, and this gambling indulgence in sports lottery has resulted in his losing everything.
Habituated is in the closest meaning to this word.
A. facilitated   C. addicted
B. cynical   D. suspicious

278. Dinosaurs _____ sixty-five million years ago, but for unknown reasons, either the hit of an asteroid or comet or the sudden freezing cold climate, the once master of the world got wiped out.
Survived is in the closest meaning to this word.
A. absorbed   C. devastated
B. existed   D. fluctuated

279. With strong _____conscience in mind, the author wrote novels only about the themes of ecology, human harmony, and universal truths.
Societal is in the closest meaning to this word.
A. social   C. radioactive
B. indigenous   D. explanatory

280. Melissa was optimistic about her getting the new job, for her qualifications and experience perfectly fit the required _____ for it.

Qualifications is in the closest meaning to this word.
A. fraud
C. vividness
B. prestige
D. eligibility

277. 亞瑟無可救藥地沉迷於運動賭博，而這種運動彩券的賭癮導致他失去一切。
Habituated 的意思最接近於這個字。
A. 促進
C. **上癮**
B. 冷嘲的
D. 懷疑的

278. 恐龍曾經存在於六千五百萬年前，但是因為不明的原因，也許是小流星或是彗星的撞擊，也或許是氣候的驟降，一度是世界的主宰者就這樣被滅絕了。
Survived 的意思最接近於這個字。
A. 吸收
C. 毀滅
B. **存在**
D. 波動

279. 有著強烈的社會良知，這名作家只寫有關於生態環境、人類和諧，以及普世真理這類主題的小說。
Societal 的意思最接近於這個字。
A. **社會的**
C. 輻射的
B. 本土的
D. 說明的

280. 梅麗莎對於得到新工作感到十分樂觀，因為她的資歷和經驗十分符合這份工作所要求的條件。
Qualifications 的意思最接近於這個字。
A. 詐欺
C. 逼真
B. 聲望
D. **資格**

答案 277. C　278. B　279. A　280. D

281. Like all _____, Ken planned to move away and live independently as soon as he entered college, and would still maintain close ties with his family.
Youths is in the closest meaning to this word.
A. linguists   C. hijackers
B. folks   D. youngsters

282. The real estate business was _____ in the past, but not now. Due to the economic recession and soaring high prices, houses are no more affordable to most people.
Flourishing is in the closest meaning to this word.
A. blooming   C. sponsored
B. thrifty   D. overdue

283. To attract students to make use of it, the school library provides all kinds of facilities for them to _____ and it also regularly holds activities.
Use is in the closest meaning to this word.
A. preserve   C. access
B. interfere   D. recruit

284. In modern days, with their multi-functional characteristics, _____ phones have become a must-have kind of equipment to most people.
Movable is in the closest meaning to this word.
A. visual   C. magnetic
B. mobile   D. artificial

281. 如同所有的年輕人，肯恩計畫一上大學就離家獨自生活，而仍舊會和家人保持密切聯繫。
Youths 的意思最接近於這個字。
A. 語言學家　　　C. 劫持者
B. 父母親　　　　**D. 年輕人**

282. 房地產事業在過去是興盛的行業，但是現在不如以往了。由於經濟不景氣以及高漲的房價，房子對大多數人來說已經不再負擔得起。
Flourishing 的意思最接近於這個字。
A. 興旺的　　　C. 贊助的
B. 節儉的　　　　D. 逾期的

283. 為了吸引學生多多利用資源，學校圖書館提供各種供他們使用的便利設施，並且也定期地舉辦活動。
Use 的意思最接近於這個字。
A. 保存　　　　　**C. 利用**
B. 干涉　　　　　D. 招募

284. 就現代而言，有著多功能的特點，手機對大多數人來說已經成為一項必備品。
Movable 的意思最接近於這個字。
A. 視覺的　　　　C. 磁鐵的
B. 移動的　　　D. 人造的

答案　**281.** D　**282.** A　**283.** C　**284.** B

285. Mozart was a brilliant and productive composer. He showed his musical talents at three, had his piano concert tour in Europe since six, and was thus praised as the classical music child _____.
Genius is in the closest meaning to this word.
A. architect   C. prodigy
B. workaholic   D. spectator

286. In his book, On the Origin of Species, Charles Darwin proposed the theory of evolution by natural _____, in which the species best suited to their environments survive and reproduce.
Choice is in the closest meaning to this word.
A. potential   C. breakdown
B. stimulation   D. selection

287. After the seminar, all the participants were asked to _____ a questionnaire to offer their opinions for further assessments.
Finish is in the closest meaning to this word.
A. complete   C. publish
B. resemble   D. admonish

288. Since 2010, the Sherlock Holmes TV series produced by BBC have successfully reinterpreted the old Holmes as a modern super detective and thus attracted _____ Sherlock fans.
Global is in the closest meaning to this word.
A. magical   C. external
B. worldwide   D. provincial

285. 莫札特是傑出且多產的作曲家。他在三歲時便展現他的音樂才華，
六歲起就在歐洲巡迴演奏鋼琴，因此被世人讚譽為古典音樂神童。
Genius 的意思最接近於這個字。
A. 建築師　　　　C. **天才**
B. 工作狂　　　　D. 觀眾

286. 查爾斯・達爾文在他的書《物種起源》中提出物競天擇的進化論，
說明適者生存，不適者淘汰的理論。
Choice 的意思最接近於這個字。
A. 潛力　　　　　C. 崩潰
B. 刺激　　　　　D. **選擇**

287. 研討會過後，所有的參加人員被要求填寫一份問卷，提供意見以做
日後評估使用。
Finish 的意思最接近於這個字。
A. **完成**　　　　C. 出版
B. 相像　　　　　D. 告誡

288. 自 2010 年以來，英國廣播公司製作的福爾摩斯電視影集成功地再度
詮釋舊式的福爾摩斯為現代超級偵探，因而吸引了世界各地的福爾
摩斯迷。
Global 的意思最接近於這個字。
A. 神奇的　　　　C. 外部的
B. **全世界的**　　D. 偏狹的

答案 285. C　286. D　287. A　288. B

模擬試題（二十五）

✏ Vocabulary in Context

MP3 025

289. The _____ of dengue fever is mainly through mosquitoes. The symptoms may include a high fever, headache, vomiting, muscle and joint pains, and a skin rash.

Spreading is in the closest meaning to this word.

A. curriculum C. performance

B. announcement D. transmission

290. While the workers were renovating the house, all the neighbors around could feel the _____ from the drilling machines operating inside.

Shaking is in the closest meaning to this word.

A. control C. phenomenon

B. vibrations D. moments

291. Euthanasia, or mercy killing, is a highly controversial issue and has long been _____ from either the medical or the ethical point of view.

Debated is in the closest meaning to this word.

A. disputed C. flourished

B. constructed D. provided

292. Mr. Webb decided to see the cardiologist because recently his chest pains came and went, which could _____ the warning of heart problems.

Indicate is in the closest meaning to this word.
A. rotate   C. signal
B. hazard   D. overwhelm

289. 登革熱的傳染主要是經由蚊子。症狀包含高燒、頭疼、嘔吐、肌肉和關節疼痛，以及皮膚紅疹。
Spreading 的意思最接近於這個字。
A. 課程   C. 表現
B. 宣佈   D. **傳染**

290. 當工人正在整修房子的時候，所有附近的鄰居都可以感受到屋內鑽孔機操作的震動。
Shaking 的意思最接近於這個字。
A. 控制   C. 現象
B. **震動**   D. 時刻

291. 安樂死是一個具高度爭議性的議題，無論是從醫學觀點或是道德觀點來說都一直受到爭論。
Debated 的意思最接近於這個字。
A. **爭論**   C. 興盛
B. 建造   D. 提供

292. 韋伯先生決定去看心臟科醫生，因為最近他的胸口不時地隱隱作痛，而這種症狀可能是心臟疾病示警的訊號。
Indicate 的意思最接近於這個字。
A. 旋轉   C. **示警**
B. 危害   D. 壓倒

答案 289. D   290. B   291. A   292. C

293. The consumers made bitter complaints about the awful food and service the restaurant offered. After the _____ took an immediate make-up action, the satisfied customers stopped further protests.
Boss is in the closest meaning to this word.
A. heir   C. conqueror
B. manager   D. retailer

294. CNBLUE, a South Korean pop rock band, released their _____ Japanese mini-album Now or Never in 2009.
First is in the closest meaning to this word.
A. splendor   C. debut
B. advent   D. revenue

295. In Greek mythology, *Pandora's Box* refers to the story that though warned against opening the box with evils inside, Pandora, out of _____, still opened it, which resulted in serious consequences.
Inquisitiveness is in the closest meaning to this word.
A. formality   C. innovation
B. redemption   D. curiosity

296. As a _____ CEO, Mark Zuckerberg, the co-founder of Facebook, remains plain, modest, and generous all the time. He never hesitates to help the world, especially children of the following generations.
Rich is in the closest meaning to this word.
A. wealthy   C. rhythmic
B. clumsy   D. indigenous

293. 這群消費者對於這家餐廳所提供劣質的食物和服務提出強烈的不滿。在經理採取立即的補救後，滿意的顧客才停止進一步的抗議。

Boss 的意思最接近於這個字。

A. 繼承人　　　C. 征服者

B. **經理**　　　D. 零售商

294. 南韓搖滾樂團，CNBLUE，在 2009 年發行他們的首張日文迷你專輯，Now or Never。

First 的意思最接近於這個字。

A. 光輝　　　　C. **初次登場**

B. 到臨　　　　D. 總收入

295. 希臘神話故事中，《潘朵拉的盒子》描述的故事內容是儘管潘朵拉被警告不能打開充滿禍害的盒子，但是由於好奇，她還是打開了盒子，最終導致嚴重的後果。

Inquisitiveness 的意思最接近於這個字。

A. 規範　　　　C. 創新

B. 贖罪　　　　D. **好奇心**

296. 臉書的共同創辦人，馬克‧祖克伯，身為富有的總裁，卻一直保持樸實、謙虛，以及慷慨的風範。他毫不猶豫地幫助全世界，尤其是未來世代的孩童。

Rich 的意思最接近於這個字。

A. **富有的**　　　C. 節奏的

B. 笨拙的　　　　D. 本地的

答案　**293.** B　**294.** C　**295.** D　**296.** A

Part 1 同義字模擬試題

Part 2 填空題模擬試題

Part 3 聽、讀整合能力強化

297. Receiving the full family _____ financially and spiritually, Paul opened a restaurant of his own and achieved prosperous business.
Aid is in the closest meaning to this word.
A. penalty   C. support
B. attitude   D. fabrication

298. Billy was newly appointed head of the market development _____ and was in charge of the research and development of his company's new products.
Division is in the closest meaning to this word.
A. chamber   C. modification
B. sequence   D. department

299. The _____ invention during the 1960s was the Internet, which was originally started by the US government for military purposes. Nowadays, people can use the Net for millions of things everywhere at any time.
Significant is in the closest meaning to this word.
A. perpetual   C. comparative
B. epochal   D. sufficient

300. To reduce the impact of global warming, scientists have been developing alternative energy resources such as _____ or wind power energy.
Sun is in the closest meaning to this word.
A. solar   C. lunar
B. artificial   D. ultraviolet

297. 得到家人全面經濟和精神上的支援，保羅開了一家自己的餐廳，並且經營地生意興隆。

Aid 的意思最接近於這個字。

A. 處罰　　　　　C. **支持**
B. 態度　　　　　D. 虛構

298. 比利最近被任命為市場開發部的主任，負責公司新產品的研究及開發的工作。

Division 的意思最接近於這個字。

A. 房間　　　　　C. 修改
B. 系列　　　　　D. **部門**

299. 60 年代意義最重大的發明就是網際網路，起初是美國政府為了軍事目的而研發的。今日而言，人們可以在任何地方、任何時刻利用網際網路做上百萬件事情。

Significant 的意思最接近於這個字。

A. 永久的　　　　C. 比較的
B. **劃時代的**　　D. 足夠的

300. 為了減緩全球暖化的衝擊，科學家一直在研發像是太陽能或是風力發電的替代能源。

Sun 的意思最接近於這個字。

A. **太陽的**　　　C. 月亮的
B. 人造的　　　　D. 紫外線的

答案　**297.** C　**298.** D　**299.** B　**300.** A

模擬試題（二十六）

Vocabulary in Context

301. The Internet enables customers to log on the online banking websites and achieve all the financial operations without going to banking _____ in person.
Organizations is in the closest meaning to this word.
A. landmarks
C. institutions
B. museums
D. workshops

302. Daniel made great fortunes from his overseas _____ and was able to fulfill his wishes of helping stray animals as much as possible.
Speculation is in the closest meaning to this word.
A. investments
C. assignments
B. editorials
D. trademarks

303. It was quite a coincidence that Madeline and Chester arrived at the award ceremony _____.
Meantime is in the closest meaning to this word.
A. legally
C. essentially
B. awkwardly
D. simultaneously

304. Austin was clever enough to take the _____; he made self-recommendation and finally got the contract of one year's work.
Lead is in the closest meaning to this word.
A. security
C. transformation
B. initiative
D. metabolism

301. 網際網路讓顧客可以不用親自前往銀行機構而是登入銀行的網站就可以完成所有的金融作業。

Organizations 的意思最接近於這個字。

A. 陸標　　　　C. **機構**

B. 博物館　　　D. 工作坊

302. 丹尼爾從海外投資賺得不少錢，因此有能力實現盡力幫助流浪動物的心願。

Speculation 的意思最接近於這個字。

A. **投資**　　　C. 任務

B. 社論　　　　D. 商標

303. 梅德琳和切斯特兩人很湊巧地同時抵達頒獎典禮的現場。

Meantime 的意思最接近於這個字。

A. 合法地　　　C. 實質上

B. 尷尬地　　　D. **同時地**

304. 奧斯丁很聰明地採取主動；他自我推薦並因此最終得到一整年的工作合約。

Lead 的意思最接近於這個字。

A. 安全　　　　C. 轉變

B. **主動**　　　D. 新陳代謝

答案　**301.** C　**302.** A　**303.** D　**304.** B

305. To maintain health, a balanced diet, regular exercise, and yearly physical check-up are essential. Above all, don't feel _____ to consult the doctor whenever there're unhealthy symptoms or health concerns.
Uncertain is in the closest meaning to this word.
A. hesitant   C. precious
B. risky   D. hospitable

306. Through excellent teamwork, Ian's group finally won the world championship by defeating all other international competitors _____.
Overpoweringly is in the closest meaning to this word.
A. confidentially   C. overwhelmingly
B. originally   D. vertically

307. The game software market has become more and more _____, and all the game programmers in the company are exerting their utmost to come up with the best designing works.
Rivaling is in the closest meaning to this word.
A. abnormal   C. surplus
B. inhabitable   D. competitive

308. As travel addicts, Ernie and Ray had the same craziness for traveling abroad, but they would travel to Western and Eastern countries _____.
Separately is in the closest meaning to this word.
A. misleadingly   C. snobbishly
B. respectively   D. profitably

305. 要保持健康，均衡的飲食、規律的運動，以及年度健康檢查是必要的。尤其 是任何刻察覺到有不健康的症狀或有健康上的疑慮時，不要遲疑於看醫生。

Uncertain 的意思最接近於這個字。

A. **猶豫的**　　　C. 珍貴的

B. 冒險的　　　　D. 好客的

306. 藉由絕佳的團隊合作，依恩的團隊壓倒性地打敗所有其他的國際參賽者，終於獲得世界冠軍。

Overpoweringly 的意思最接近於這個字。

A. 機密地　　　　C. **壓倒性地**

B. 原來地　　　　D. 垂直地

307. 遊戲軟體市場變得越來越競爭了，所有公司裡的遊戲程式設計師目前都盡力提出最優質的設計作品。

Rivaling 的意思最接近於這個字。

A. 反常的　　　　C. 過剩的

B. 適於居住的　　D. **競爭的**

308. 身為旅遊愛好者，爾尼和雷伊對於國外旅遊具有相同的熱愛，但是他們會分別前往不同的西方和東方國家旅遊。

Separately 的意思最接近於這個字。

A. 誤導地　　　　C. 勢利地

B. **分別地**　　　D. 盈利地

答案　**305.** A　**306.** C　**307.** D　**308.** B

309. While in Peru, the tour guide _____ us around the ancient Machu Picchu. Though a UNESCO World Heritage Site, due to over-tourism, it is now facing potential dangers and threats.

Led is in the closest meaning to this word.

A. conducted   C. supervised

B. oppressed   D. accumulated

310. One possible way to protect the valuable antiques of ancient times in poor countries from black-market _____ is to lease the artifacts to museums.

Deals is in the closest meaning to this word.

A. schedules   C. transactions

B. monuments   D. characteristics

311. The manager had trouble _____ the marketing reforms in the beginning, but he still held an optimistic attitude toward the prospects of success.

Executing is in the closest meaning to this word.

A. drifting   C. conflicting

B. purifying   D. implementing

312. What _____ Linda's interest in learning oil painting was her constant visiting the art museum and appreciating lots of artistic works.

Stimulated is in the closest meaning to this word.

A. opposed   C. communicated

B. aroused   D. acknowledged

309. 在祕魯時，導遊引導我們在馬丘比丘古城旅遊。雖然是一個聯合國教科文組織世界文化遺跡所在地，由於過度觀光，它目前正面臨潛在的危險和威脅。

Led 的意思最接近於這個字。

A. **引導**　　C. 監督
B. 壓迫　　　D. 累積

310. 一個保護貧窮國家古代珍貴的古董免於黑市買賣的可能方法是把這些手工藝品租借給博物館。

Deals 的意思最接近於這個字。

A. 預定行程　　C. **交易**
B. 紀念碑　　　D. 特徵

311. 這名經理在剛開始實施行銷改革上遭逢困難，但他對於成功的願景仍舊抱持著樂觀的態度。

Executing 的意思最接近於這個字。

A. 漂流　　C. 衝突
B. 淨化　　D. **實施**

312. 激發琳達學習畫油畫的興趣是因為她經常參觀美術館並且欣賞許多藝術畫作。

Stimulated 的意思最接近於這個字。

A. 反對　　　C. 溝通
B. **激發**　　D. 承認

答案 309. A　310. C　311. D　312. B

模擬試題（二十七）

✏ Vocabulary in Context MP3 027

313. Though eccentric, the future king actually has deep passions. He maintains his royal _____ successfully by his devotion to the royal family and warm care about his dear nation.
Symbol is in the closest meaning to this word.
A. authority   C. comprehension
B. image   D. sympathy

314. The custom-made computer desk is not only functional in usage but easy to handle because of its _____ wheels.
Shiftable is in the closest meaning to this word.
A. fierce   C. movable
B. vulnerable   D. complacent

315. The increasing _____ of operating processes in the factory achieved high productivity and considerable profits at low costs.
Automation is in the closest meaning to this word.
A. obedience   C. nourishment
B. precaution   D. mechanization

316. Using the power of music, painting the ideas that come easily, and taking down notes of the original ideas are what kept the _____ artist creative.

Prolific is in the closest meaning to this word.
A. urgent   C. productive
B. excessive   D. transparent

---

313. 雖然脾氣古怪，這位未來的國王事實上有著強烈的熱情。他透過對於皇室家族的奉獻以及對他摯愛國家溫馨的關切得以成功地維護他的皇室形象。

Symbol 的意思最接近於這個字。
A. 權威   C. 理解
B. 形象   D. 同情

---

314. 這張客製化的電腦桌不僅在使用上具多重功能，可移動的輪子也使得它易於操作。

Shiftable 的意思最接近於這個字。
A. 兇猛的   **C. 活動的**
B. 脆弱的   D. 自滿的

---

315. 工廠裡操作過程逐漸增加的機械化程度得以低成本達到高生產力以及大量的利潤。

Automation 的意思最接近於這個字。
A. 服從   C. 營養
B. 預防措施   **D. 機械化**

---

316. 利用音樂的力量、繪出油然而生的靈感，並且記載下原創的思維是促使這位多產藝術家保有創意的方法。

Prolific 的意思最接近於這個字。
A. 緊急的   **C. 多產的**
B. 過度的   D. 透明的

答案 **313.** B   **314.** C   **315.** D   **316.** C

317. When it comes to happiness, wealth alone is not necessarily _____ with it. In fact, health, knowledge, and family should also be included.
Equivalent is in the closest meaning to this word.
A. audible
C. bewildering
B. synonymous
D. miserable

318. The CEO is a successful businessman with a breadth of vision; both his domestic and foreign _____ have been increasing and prosperous.
Ventures is in the closest meaning to this word.
A. reforms
C. approaches
B. lectures
D. enterprises

319. The Emperor Qin Shi Huang was an important historical figure in China, for during the third century BC, he _____ the warring China, the Chinese written language, and the systems of laws and weights.
Uniformed is in the closest meaning to this word.
A. unified
C. deprived
B. abused
D. prosecuted

320. To achieve fairness, the teacher _____ her grades of evaluating students' performances in both the overall behavior and their academic works.
Unified is in the closest meaning to this word.
A. conflicted
C. standardized
B. abandoned
D. estimated

317. 論到快樂，單有財富未必等同於幸福。事實上，健康、知識，以及家庭也應該包括在內。
Equivalent 的意思最接近於這個字。
A. 可聽見的 　　　 C. 困惑的
B. **同義的** 　　　 D. 悲慘的

318. 這名總裁是一位眼光廣闊，事業有成的企業家；他國內以及國外的企業一直在擴張並且蒸蒸日上。
Ventures 的意思最接近於這個字。
A. 改革 　　　 C. 方法
B. 講課 　　　 D. **企業**

319. 秦始皇在中國是一位重要的歷史人物，因為在西元前三世紀期間，他統一了戰亂的中國、中國文字，以及法律和度量衡的制度。
Uniformed 的意思最接近於這個字。
A. **統一** 　　　 C. 剝奪
B. 濫用 　　　 D. 起訴

320. 為了達到公平，這名老師訂定統一標準，以學生整體的行為表現以及他們的學術成績作為評分的標準。
Unified 的意思最接近於這個字。
A. 衝突 　　　 C. **標準化**
B. 放棄 　　　 D. 預測

答案 **317.** B 　 **318.** D 　 **319.** A 　 **320.** C

321. Ever since Robin _____ great fortunes from his parents, he quit his job and pursued material joyfulness, such as buying fancy sports cars and living in luxurious mansions.
Received is in the closest meaning to this word.
A. inherited   C. subsided
B. penalized   D. assembled

322. Lacking convincing witnesses and concrete _____, the police could not but release the probable murderer, who provided an airtight alibi for the time of the crime.
Proof is in the closest meaning to this word.
A. budget   C. observation
B. evidence   D. transmission

323. With their _____ characteristics, the products of this company have been very popular both in the mall and on the Internet.
Adaptable is in the closest meaning to this word.
A. panic   C. ventilating
B. subsequent   D. adjustable

324. The high living costs and the low pay forced Tom to live an _____ life, which brought about lots of complaints from his wife and children.
Thrifty is in the closest meaning to this word.
A. ignorant   C. economical
B. persuasive   D. uneventful

321. 自從羅賓繼承雙親龐大的遺產後，他辭職去追求物質的享受，譬如購買豪華跑車以及住奢華的房子。
Received 的意思最接近於這個字。
A. **繼承**　　　C. 消退
B. 處罰　　　D. 組裝

322. 由於缺乏可信的目擊證人以及具體的證據，警方不得不釋放涉案成份高的謀殺犯，因為他提出案發當時完美的不在場證明。。
Proof 的意思最接近於這個字。
A. 預算　　　C. 觀察
B. **證據**　　　D. 輸送

323. 這家公司的產品由於具有可調整的特色，在大賣場以及網路上一向頗受歡迎。
Adaptable 的意思最接近於這個字。
A. 恐慌的　　　C. 通風的
B. 後續的　　　D. **可調整的**

324. 高額的生活費用以及低廉的薪資迫使湯姆過著節儉的生活，卻因此導致妻子和孩子許多的抱怨。
Thrifty 的意思最接近於這個字。
A. 無知的　　　C. **節約的**
B. 說服的　　　D. 平靜無事的

答案　**321.** A　**322.** B　**323.** D　**324.** C

模擬試題（二十八）

✎ Vocabulary in Context

MP3 028

325. When the Nobel Peace Prize-Winner, Dr. King, delivered his famous speech, I Have a Dream, to tell of his dream land of equality, a large _____ of whites and blacks were attracted to share and support his ideals.
Spectators is in the closest meaning to this word.
A. choir   C. audience
B. staff   D. pantheon

326. With the release of his new single album, the reggae singer and songwriter believed that he was on his way to becoming a _____ name.
Family is in the closest meaning to this word.
A. household   C. prelude
B. resource   D. fulfillment

327. To Natalie, it has been her lifelong ambition to enter the _____ business, become a celebrity, and make huge amounts of money.
Show is in the closest meaning to this word.
A. egoism   C. transportation
B. judgment   D. entertainment

328. Starting as an _____ writer, Ryan set up high standards and goals, took an active attitude, and worked non-stop to become professional in his field.

Inexperienced is in the closest meaning to this word.
A. external   C. uncultured
B. amateur   D. institutional

325. 當諾貝爾和平獎得主，金恩博士，發表他著名的演說，《我有一個夢想》，描述他平等的夢想國度時，大群受到吸引的白人及黑人聽眾前來分享並支持他的理念。
Spectators 的意思最接近於這個字。
A. 合唱隊   **C. 觀眾**
B. 職員   D. 眾神

326. 隨著他最新單曲的發行，這名雷鬼歌手兼作曲家相信他即將成為家喻戶曉的名歌手。
Family 的意思最接近於這個字。
A. 家庭   C. 前奏曲
B. 資源   D. 實現

327. 對娜塔莉來說，她終生的抱負就是要進入演藝圈、成為名流，並且賺大錢。
Show 的意思最接近於這個字。
A. 自我主義   C. 交通運輸
B. 判斷   **D. 娛樂**

328. 以一名業餘的作家起家，雷恩訂定崇高的標準和目標、採取主動的態度，並且不斷地工作，目標是要成為他領域中的專業人士。
Inexperienced 的意思最接近於這個字。
A. 外部的   C. 未受教育的
B. 業餘的   D. 制度的

答案　**325.** C　**326.** A　**327.** D　**328.** B

329. Most modern consumers are environmental-minded enough to choose highly energy- _____ and healthful products to purchase.
Economical is in the closest meaning to this word.
A. efficient   C. sensational
B. contagious   D. fundamental

330. It was insensible and irresponsible of Mr. Watt's family to _____ the treatment of his cancer and took him home from the hospital.
Stop is in the closest meaning to this word.
A. propel   C. discontinue
B. ascertain   D. compensate

331. Steven's family and friends were truly unable to _____ why he should have given up the chance of entering a more prestigious university.
Understand is in the closest meaning to this word.
A. despise   C. withdraw
B. grasp   D. enlighten

332. The senior supervisor commented that there was still much room left to be desired, which showed the _____ that he wasn't satisfied with the results and we'd better work harder.
Hint is in the closest meaning to this word.
A. outlet   C. measurement
B. elevation   D. implication

329. 大多數現代的消費者具有足夠的環保意識去選擇購買高效節能以及健康的產品。

Economical 的意思最接近於這個字。

A. **有效率的**　　C. 轟動的

B. 傳染性的　　　D. 基礎的

330. 瓦特先生的家人十分不明智並且不負責任地終止他癌症的治療，並將他從醫院帶回家。

Stop 的意思最接近於這個字。

A. 推進　　　　C. **中斷**

B. 查明　　　　D. 賠償

331. 史蒂芬的家人和朋友真的無法理解為何他竟然放棄了可以進入更具卓越聲譽大學的機會。

Understand 的意思最接近於這個字。

A. 鄙視　　　　C. 撤回

B. **理解**　　　D. 啟發

332. 高層主管評論説仍有極大的改善空間，這暗示著他對於結果並不滿意，我們最好更加努力些。

Hint 的意思最接近於這個字。

A. 銷路　　　　C. 測量

B. 提高　　　　D. **暗示**

答案　**329.** A　**330.** C　**331.** B　**332.** D

333. The reports of the investigation _____ the fact that the mayor was behind all these illegal public property deals.
Disclosed is in the closest meaning to this word.
A. refunded   C. embarked
B. unveiled   D. preached

334. Due to drunk driving and breaking the speed limit, the driver was brought to the police station for serious traffic _____.
Law-breaking is in the closest meaning to this word.
A. twist   C. violation
B. rehearsal   D. collaboration

335. After exploring every possible _____, the team finally came up with a good solution and succeeded in achieving the mission.
Means is in the closest meaning to this word.
A. avenue   C. network
B. diversion   D. recollection

336. Depressed with huge debts and bad health, Mr. Haydn ended up being a chronic _____ and had to be sent to a rehabilitation clinic for cure.
Drunkard is in the closest meaning to this word.
A. rival   C. proponent
B. specialist   D. alcoholic

333. 調查報告揭露的事實顯示是市長主導所有這些非法的公有房地產交易。

Disclosed 的意思最接近於這個字。

A. 退款　　　　C. 裝載

B. 揭露　　　D. 佈道

334. 由於酒駕以及超速，這名駕駛因嚴重的交通違規被帶至警局。

Low-breaking 的意思最接近於這個字。

A. 扭曲　　　　**C. 違規**

B. 排練　　　　D. 合作

335. 在探索所有可能的方法後，這個團隊終於提出絕佳的解決方案並且成功地完成任務。

Means 的意思最接近於這個字。

A. **方法**　　　C. 網路

B. 轉向　　　　D. 回憶

336. 海頓先生由於高額的債務以及不良的健康狀況深受打擊，最終結果是成為一名慢性酒精中毒者，並且必須送到戒酒康復診所尋求治療。

Drunkard 的意思最接近於這個字。

A. 對手　　　　C. 擁護者

B. 專家　　　　**D. 嗜酒者**

答案　**333.** B　　**334.** C　　**335.** A　　**336.** D

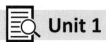

The Internet's **1.** _____ among adolescents brought about serious academic and personality problems and has gradually aroused social attention.

The refined merchandise exhibited in the Trade Fair last month was **2.** _____ by Morrison Company and has received great numbers of orders since then.

After surviving the horrible plane crash, Pamela came to realize the value of life and was **3.** _____ to social charity causes.

is in the closest meaning to this word.

It is **4.** _____ that producing books in hard copy format may bring several million tons of harmful CO2 into the atmosphere, so E-books are definitely here to stay.

Young generations should be taught from their early childhood to practice the 3R **5.** _____ — Reduce, Reuse, and Recycle to protect and sustain the earth.

Animal rights groups **6.** _____ to take more drastic measures unless the cosmetic manufactures stopped inhumane animal tests.

The company has recently renewed the computer software, and is working on tests to make sure the new system will be **7.** _____ with the existing apparatus.

Martin has lived in comfort and luxury ever since he made successful **8.** _____ investments and piled up a considerable fortune.

Given that dust storms have been **9.** _____ in huge amounts with greater forces, scientists all over the world are working on the causes and the solutions.

Thanks to the decreased costs of 3D printers, the technology of the three-dimensional printing has recently gained **10.** _____ among different fields of industry.

Mr. Banks is a lawyer **11.** _____ in criminal laws and is dedicated to defending against criminal charges.

Mrs. Newman planned to move to the countryside, following her doctor's advice that the rural environment might be conducive to the **12.** _____ of her health.

A produced	**B** compatible	**C** popularity
D restrictions	**E** estimated	**F** manufactured
G prevalence	**H** specialized	**I** recovery
J restoration	**K** dependence	**L** superstitious
M principles	**N** pecuniary	**O** claimed
P professionalized	**Q** addiction	**R** converted
S created	**T** agreeable	**U** degenerated
V changed	**W** calculated	**X** announced

Luke **13.** _____ on the idea that people should protect rare and extinct animals, and he constantly sponsored campaigns of the kind.

Electronic products **14.** _____ from Japan have always received great welcome because they tend to be functional and durable.

It's amazing that nowadays consumers can **15.** _____ almost anything through shopping websites on the Internet.

The Anderson family decided to **16.** _____ to Australia to try their luck and start a new life there.

Irene had better watch out for those her gossip friends who may once in a while **17.** _____ rumors about her.

At the present time, scientists spare no efforts to find resources of the alternative energy to substitute for the fossil fuels **18.** _____ by industry.

The manager informed the factory that they might **19.** _____ or even cancel the original orders if the goods shipped in continued to be in poor quality.

The movie adapted from a novel was disappointing to the moviegoers because they could hardly find any **20.** _____ between the two.

The **21.** _____ of technology to our daily life enables us to live comfortably and joyfully.

After most of its safety **22.** _____ failed to meet the standards, the mall was seriously penalized and had to make immediate improvement.

To keep healthy, one should be careful not to consume too much the food that **23.** _____ additives, such as preservatives, coloring, or artificial flavorings.

To make both ends meet, Roy had no choice but to take several part-time jobs to **24.** _____ additional income.

A	examination	**B**	generate	**C**	supervise
D	fastened	**E**	introduced	**F**	correspondence
G	move	**H**	ridiculed	**I**	utilization
J	digests	**K**	withhold	**L**	consistency
M	exhausted	**N**	buy	**O**	emigrate
P	contains	**Q**	decrease	**R**	purchase
S	inspections	**T**	imported	**U**	application
V	consumed	**W**	pacify	**X**	scatter

Due to the continuous bad selling condition, the company **25.** _____ that a certain percentage of the staff members had to be laid off.

Jason's bossy character and his wish to **26.** _____ over others make him the least popular person among all.

The world surrounding us is a seriously **27.** _____ one, and we must take precautions to cope with the global ecological crisis.

The applicant's additional language skills and working experience definitely **28.** _____ the chance of being employed.

To **29.** _____ the risk of clogged arteries and heart attacks, one had better get away from trans fats, which may cause the rise of cholesterol in the blood.

It's essential for every global villager to keep it in mind that we all should undertake the **30.** _____ to protect the environment for our future generations.

Dr. Martin Luther King Jr.'s **31.** _____ of non-violence in struggling against racial discrimination and segregation won him the utmost respect from the world.

The poor financial management of Mr. Smith's enterprise was responsible for his unfortunate **32.** _____ in the end.

As soon as the renowned company posted an advertisement of a position for a manager, a large number of qualified jobseekers **33.** _____ for the job.

It is imperative that we humans put emphasis on ecological **34.** _____ and set up as many wildlife reserves as we can.

All those present were bothered by the intruder, who both inappropriately dressed himself and rudely behaved on the solemn **35.** _____.

Though careful with the budget, with the soaring high living costs, Michael's expenses invariably **36.** _____ his income every month.

Part 1 同義字模擬試題

Part 2 填空題模擬試題

Part 3 聽、讀整合能力強化

A announced	**B** control	**C** failure
D monitored	**E** obligation	**F** dominate
G polluted	**H** decrease	**I** hospitality
J preservation	**K** declared	**L** contaminated
M add	**N** maintenance	**O** protection
P exceeded	**Q** increase	**R** circumstance
S surpassed	**T** utilize	**U** occasion
V administered	**W** bankruptcy	**X** advocacy

Online shoppers always find themselves get attracted by the dazzling **37.** _____ advertisements and increase the unnecessary spending.

The most **38.** _____ trip for the happy couple was the trip to Europe for their 10th Wedding Anniversary.

The serial killer's bold and **39.** _____ murdering finally resulted in his being arrested and sentenced.

DNA was **40.** _____ by a German scientist, Friedrich Miescher, in 1869. From the information in DNA, a lot about a human's family, health, and personality can be revealed.

Fanny studied and researched diligently and finally got **41.** _____ to her ideal graduate school.

Owing to the **42.** _____ resources, we must do our utmost to come up with practical measures for sustainable development.

We are fortunate to live in an era of convenience and information. Through the far-reaching Internet, we can easily get **43.** _____ with the world.

According to medical researches, nuts are very **44.** _____ at lowering cholesterol levels and preventing heart and blood vessel diseases.

When writing his doctoral thesis, Frank made good use of the **45.** _____ facilities in the school library and finally got graduated with honors.

Scientists have found that the music that Mozart composed and **46.** _____ has a miraculous healing and calming effect to its listeners.

You can of course contact a travel agency to make travel arrangements for you; one **47.** _____ to this is that you and your family can organize your own trip.

Richard was the "Workaholic" in his office because he always kept himself busy and was fully **48.** _____ in his work.

A discovered	**B** consented	**C** restricted
D mercantile	**E** effective	**F** obtainable
G connected	**H** memorable	**I** played
J preferred	**K** submerged	**L** limited
M alternative	**N** ceaseless	**O** depreciation
P commercial	**Q** unforgettable	**R** admitted
S condensed	**T** available	**U** continuous
V occupied	**W** nimble	**X** performed

Due to her thoughtful personality and language capability, Lydia was fully qualified as a competent flight **49.** _____.

The ancient Machu Picchu used to be a summer resort for Incan emperors and their **50.** _____ family.

In the action movie, the superheroes, with each of whom equipped with combating skills, finally won the victory with **51.** _____ forces.

Undoubtedly, it is the parents that should strictly regulate their children not to watch TV programs that are too **52.** _____ in violence.

As a safety policy against terrorism, all passengers are **53.** _____ to undergo and pass the strict security check at the airport.

The publicity campaign did much to **54.** _____ the new product, promoting its unexpected big sale.

What the general public expects from the government is a **55.** _____ economic development that it is supposed to achieve.

A lot of celebrities dressed up and attended the party tonight to support the charity campaign that was **56.** _____ by the association.

The news reporter purchased the newest laptop computer **57.** _____ for the purpose of covering instant news.

Doctors warned people against the long **58.** _____ to the burning sunlight, which might easily cause skin cancer.

The candidate suffered a serious setback when the newsweekly **59.** _____ a series of disgraceful scandals about his family.

Mother Teresa's lifelong devotion to the welfare of people and the advocacy of humanity won worldwide **60.** _____ and was awarded the Nobel Peace Prize in 1979.

A detective	**B** steady	**C** advertise
D particularly	**E** royal	**F** specifically
G supreme	**H** realistic	**I** uncovered
J worshipped	**K** started	**L** imperial
M launched	**N** lifelike	**O** popularize
P accusation	**Q** waterproof	**R** revealed
S dominant	**T** demanded	**U** exposure
V recognition	**W** stewardess	**X** uncovering

In America, young people will often move out and live an **61.** _____ life when they turn eighteen or go to college.

Those naughty students were insistently requested to make a(n) **62.** _____ of their misbehavior, or they might receive a severe punishment.

According to TV reports, the sending out of the **63.** _____ gas and fumes of the factory might be the cause of the serious sickness of the residents.

Carlos bought an apartment near the MRT station as he considered it **64.** _____ and time-saving for him to commute by MRT.

The corporation planned to establish chain stores all over the world and made great efforts to look for superior and **65.** _____ store managers.

The factory was forced to slow down its manufacturing speed after parts of its **66.** _____ apparatus went wrong.

To achieve the sustainability of the earth and humans, it's essential that we cherish and conserve the **67.** _____ natural ecosystems.

The notorious mayor, who committed bribery and embezzlement, finally handed in his **68.** _____ and was put in jail.

To **69.** _____ a higher level of education is vital to getting better employment and fairer salaries in the future.

People all over the world used to view the United States as a land of golden **70.** _____ and tried their luck by emigrating there.

Little did we expect that the minor misunderstanding between the couple should have **71.** _____ caused them to break up.

Talking too loudly on a cell phone may cause disturbance to people around you, **72.** _____ in a cinema.

A	trustworthy	**B**	autonomous	**C**	undeveloped
D	obtain	**E**	independent	**F**	unexploited
G	poisonous	**H**	alteration	**I**	receive
J	chance	**K**	corrections	**L**	especially
M	unexpectedly	**N**	architectural	**O**	opportunity
P	reliable	**Q**	quitting	**R**	handy
S	righteously	**T**	resignation	**U**	dramatically
V	mechanical	**W**	therapeutic	**X**	convenient

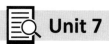

The admirable NBA basketball players are not only **73.** _____ in their basketball skills but passionate and generous in supporting charity work.

The board of directors announced several measures to minimize the problem to a more **74.** _____ level.

The painful bothering and torments to celebrities and the **75.** _____ are the endless pursuit and photographing of the paparazzi.

It's generally believed that during the fourth century B.C., Alexander the Great **76.** _____ the arrival of perfume in Greece.

Due to **77.** _____ serious delays of shipment, the company decided to ask for compensation or even a full refund.

Out of pity, Rick **78.** _____ the old man who seemed to have lost his way to the police station and helped him return home.

Recently, a team of scientists, teachers, and students went on an **79.** _____ to explore some of the wonders of the Amazon Rainforest.

The **80.** _____ expressions the professor used made it easier for the students to comprehend the difficult theories.

As soon as Steven got his year-end bonus, he purchased a highly functional digital camera that could adjust **81.** _____.

The real estate prices brought up by rich investors recently have become hardly **82.** _____, especially to young people with low income.

The police tried to find the true murderer by **83.** _____ the suspects one by one through investigation.

The heavy casualties on the superhighway last weekend resulted from the serious chain **84.** _____ among seven cars, accompanied by terrifying car-burning afterward.

A	well-trained	**B**	numerous	**C**	journey
D	irrelevantly	**E**	meditated	**F**	condensed
G	nobles	**H**	eliminating	**I**	Buyable
J	escorted	**K**	manageable	**L**	expedition
M	smashing	**N**	standardizing	**O**	accompanied
P	royalty	**Q**	controllable	**R**	simplified
S	spontaneously	**T**	deceiving	**U**	affordable
V	many	**W**	presented	**X**	professional

The tragic sinking of the British luxury liner Titanic in 1912 resulted in the heavy casualties of 1,500 deaths out of around 2,500 **85. _____**.

The sample was observed carefully under **86. _____** of 1,000 times their actual size through the powerful microscope.

The famous American jazz musician, Louis Armstrong, was not only a popular entertainer but an innovative jazz composer, who greatly **87. _____** and influenced the young music generations.

With his smooth body language, the salesman successfully **88. _____** the operation of the kitchen appliances.

It bothered Barney a lot that his wife had been such ashopaholic that their debts were worsened to a hardly **89. _____** level.

The successful writing of the magic adventures of Harry Potter by J. K. Rowling aroused the **90. _____** of readers all over the world.

On hot summer days, children and adults alike find the **91. _____** to eating refreshing ice cream too hard to break down.

The American industrialist, Henry Ford, was a **92. _____** in auto industry, who mass produced cars affordable to average people with the assembly-line technique.

We all should make every **93.** _____ to strengthen our environmental awareness and work out measures to cope with global warming.

After working in the company for ten years, Joseph decided to quit the job owing to the **94.** _____ of his enduring the heavy workload.

The distant **95.** _____ of the Pluto at the furthest reaches of the sun has always aroused astronomers' curiosity and interests to know more about it.

According to archaeologists, the **96.** _____ of the Stonehenge in Southern England was originally to serve as an observatory and an astronomical calendar.

A	legislation	**B**	refusal	**C**	revenge
D	limitation	**E**	passengers	**F**	displayed
G	enlargement	**H**	encouraged	**I**	rotation
J	resistance	**K**	intensified	**L**	inhabitants
M	magnification	**N**	fantasy	**O**	demonstrated
P	pioneer	**Q**	manageable	**R**	controllable
S	construction	**T**	endeavor	**U**	obstacle
V	victim	**W**	extremity	**X**	disillusion

Albert Einstein, the 1921 Nobel Prize winner in physics, made great **97.** _____ to the world by his Theory of Relativity, which changed mankind's understanding of science.

The entire country is going through an economic **98.** _____ and is filled with an atmosphere of uncertainty and anxiety.

It is taken for granted that you will be seriously punished if you violate the traffic **99.** _____ by driving in the wrong direction.

After going through the serious **100.** _____ conditions in the airplane last year, Mrs. Spencer claimed to avoid taking any airplanes because of the strong fear of flights.

The doctor advised the **101.** _____ to quit smoking and drinking for the sake of his health.

Mr. Emerson consulted a **102.** _____ and was prescribed some medicine for his high blood pressure.

Penicillin, a substance used as a drug to treat or prevent bacteria-caused infections, is undoubtedly the greatest **103.** _____ discovery of the 20th century.

Though Mr. Cook's health had notably **104.** _____, he remained optimistic and lighthearted for fear that his family might be sad.

Eco-minded car drivers are encouraged to purchase cars equipped with lower **105.** _____ of CO2 and hybrid engines so as to support global green revolution.

Myron was **106.** _____ as the leader of the project team and was fully dedicated to the realization of his new ideas.

With lots of photos and signatures of movie stars hung on the wall, the famous restaurant was **107.** _____ as a dining place frequented by celebrities and movie stars.

The extraordinary new Hollywood actress **108.** _____ her position as the most promising future star by her excellent performing skills and high popularity with movie fans.

A	sufferer	**B**	characterized	**C**	allocated
D	discharge	**E**	recession	**F**	consolidated
G	contributions	**H**	emissions	**I**	designated
J	therapeutic	**K**	patient	**L**	donations
M	medical	**N**	violent	**O**	declined
P	explanations	**Q**	turbulent	**R**	secured
S	executive	**T**	regulations	**U**	reproached
V	physician	**W**	depression	**X**	weakened

In the airport, hundreds of baseball fans welcomed the **109.** _____ heroes, who had just won the world championship.

The late philanthropist was kind-hearted and generous, whose charity deeds were meaningful and **110.** _____.

The **111.** _____ damage of the disaster was so large that there was no way of making any actual estimation.

In many **112.** _____ countries, lovers celebrate Valentine's Day on February 14. They give each other cards and presents like flowers and chocolate. At night, they enjoy a romantic candlelight dinner together.

The CEO read the files and discussed about the investment projects with his consultants while taking a **113.** _____ flight.

The distinguished alumnus generously left an **114.** _____ of three million dollars to the university to show his gratitude and support.

Among all the public **115.** _____ means in the city, the MRT is the most convenient and the most popular one.

The firefighters tried their best to come to the **116.** _____ of the old couple from the burning apartment, but in vain.

Bruce felt frustrated and stressed when the professor informed him of the fact that his doctoral dissertation needed considerable **117.** _____.

The **118.** _____ city in Turkey has been famous and popular for its structural and historical mystery, which attracts tourists all over the world for sightseeing.

The **119.** _____ of John F. Kennedy was one of the world's most shocking moments, and the whole nation mourned over the death of the promising young president, who was expected to accomplish great deeds.

Without doubt, the successful **120.** _____ and marketing strategies contributed to not only the popularity of Korean culture but the big sales of Korean products.

A transportation	**B** countless	**C** uncountable
D rescue	**E** pessimistic	**F** eligible
G subterranean	**H** transcontinental	**I** occidental
J optimism	**K** coordination	**L** courteous
M compatible	**N** endowment	**O** full-scale
P publicity	**Q** triumphant	**R** modification
S propaganda	**T** contribution	**U** vaccination
V assassination	**W** efficiency	**X** overall

Huge heavy motorcycles in Taiwan not only cause a lot of air **121.** _____ but disturb people in quiet neighborhoods, which arouses serious complaints from the general public.

The experience of being a part-time design **122.** _____ at night helped Gina a lot in getting official full-time employment as a formal designer after her college graduation.

Shouldering **123.** _____ responsibility to support the family, Roy couldn't but take several part-time jobs besides his regular work.

The best solution to the issue is to **124.** _____ the old prejudice and bad feelings toward each other and cooperate again.

With the health awareness prevailing, **125.** _____ foods, vegetables and fruits have been in high demand these days.

After election, Mr. Major was finally formally **126.** _____ into the office of mayor and started fulfilling his campaign promises.

The police intensively **127.** _____ possible links between the suspect and the case of suicide, in which telecommunications fraud was allegedly to have cost the victim huge amounts of his pension.

The stressful work and the chronic diseases **128.** _____ to Mr. Dewey's serious insomnia at night.

As the books in the library are **129.** _____ according to their subjects, it's easy to find the books you want.

The factory decided to modernize the **130.** _____ to meet the increasing demand of both domestic and foreign orders.

The Internet brings us a lot of access and conveniences; with only a click of the mouse, we can make collection and **131.** _____ of information easily.

Simon was experienced and well-trained in his field and was chosen as an agent to **132.** _____ the company.

A delegate	**B** assistant	**C** inaugurated
D classified	**E** helper	**F** categorized
G inducted	**H** transmission	**I** apparatus
J contamination	**K** contributed	**L** anticipate
M equipment	**N** investigated	**O** reinforcement
P miraculous	**Q** natural	**R** subscribed
S enormous	**T** complicate	**U** inspected
V pollution	**W** discard	**X** organic

Arthur was hopelessly **133.** _____ to sports betting, and this gambling indulgence in sports lottery has resulted in his losing everything.

The kidnapper **134.** _____ to kill the hostage if he didn't get the ransom.

To cope with the problems of global warming, the public are **135.** _____ to recycle and reuse everything, take the mass transportation, and use the electricity economically.

Donna and Scott were in serious **136.** _____ over cloning. The former felt that safe cloning to prolong humans' life was OK, while the later was against the idea of playing God.

137. _____ within the Bermuda Islands, the Bermuda Triangle is an area abounded by Florida, Bermuda, and Puerto Rico, where ships and planes would vanish mysteriously.

After Marvin was appointed to **138.** _____ the international conference, he devoted himself fully to accomplishing the work.

Mozart showed his musical talents at three, had his piano concert tour in Europe since six, and was thus praised as the classical music child **139.** _____.

Melissa was optimistic about her getting the new job, for her qualifications and experience perfectly fit the required **140.** _____ for it.

With the Internet **141.** _____ to us, we can achieve a lot of things; in the meantime, we should be careful not to get addicted or fall victim to net frauds.

Robots have been useful in the industry and the household. Now in Japan, they also **142.** _____ service in the medical field.

The Japanese mountaineer Junko Tabei was the first woman to conquer Mount Everest in 1975. To her, it was the willpower, together with technique and capability, that helped her **143.** _____ the impossible task.

In **144.** _____ days, making proper health management is essential since health is the foundation of success and happiness.

A	accessible	**B**	offer	**C**	argument
D	habituated	**E**	trigger	**F**	contemporary
G	qualifications	**H**	menaced	**I**	prodigy
J	addicted	**K**	arrange	**L**	situated
M	eligibility	**N**	threatened	**O**	genius
P	organize	**Q**	encouraged	**R**	located
S	accomplish	**T**	Inspired	**U**	disagreement
V	plagiarise	**W**	available	**X**	erotic

Pandora's Box refers to the story that though warned against opening the box with evils inside, Pandora, out of **145.** _____, still opened it, which resulted in serious consequences.

The **146.** _____ of dengue fever is mainly through mosquitoes. The symptoms may include a high fever, and a skin rash.

The **147.** _____ invention during the 1960s was the Internet, which was originally started by the US government for military purposes.

To reduce the impact of global warming, scientists have been developing alternative energy resources such as **148.** _____ or wind power energy.

As a **149.** _____ CEO, Mark Zuckerberg, the co-founder of Facebook, remains plain, modest, and generous all the time. He never hesitates to help the world, especially children of the following generations.

Mr. Webb decided to see the cardiologist because recently his chest pains came and went, which could **150.** _____ the warning of heart problems.

Billy was newly appointed head of the market development **151.** _____ and was in charge of the research and development of his company's new products.

Daniel made great fortunes from his overseas **152.** _____ and was able to fulfill his wishes of helping stray animals as much as possible.

To maintain health, a balanced diet, regular exercise, and yearly physical check-up are essential. Above all, don't feel **153.** _____ to consult the doctor whenever there're unhealthy symptoms or health concerns.

The game software market has become more and more **154.** _____, and all the game programmers in the company are exerting their utmost to come up with the best designing works.

While the workers were renovating the house, all the neighbors around could feel the **155.** _____ from the drilling machines operating inside.

CNBLUE, a South Korean pop rock band, released their **156.** _____ Japanese mini-album Now or Never in 2009.

A wealthy	**B** clumsy	**C** signal
D transmission	**E** inquisitiveness	**F** sufficient
G hesitant	**H** inhabitable	**I** solar
J vibrations	**K** curiosity	**L** significant
M speculation	**N** debut	**O** epochal
P investments	**Q** risky	**R** fabrication
S competitive	**T** division	**U** revenue
V indicate	**W** department	**X** abnormal

To achieve fairness, the teacher **157.** _____ her grades of evaluating students' performances in both the overall behavior and their academic works.

The emperor Qin Shi Huang was an important historical figure in China, for during the third century BC, he **158.** _____ the warring China, the Chinese written language, and the systems of laws and weights.

The increasing **159.** _____ of operating processes in the factory achieved high productivity and considerable profits at low costs.

With their **160.** _____ characteristics, the products of this company have been very popular both in the mall and on the Internet.

The high living costs and the low pay forced Tom to live an **161.** _____ life, which brought about lots of complaints from his wife and children.

When it comes to happiness, wealth alone is not necessarily **162.** _____ with it. In fact, health, knowledge, and family should also be included.

Using the power of music, painting the ideas that come easily, and taking down notes of the original ideas are what kept the **163.** _____ artist creative.

The custom-made computer desk is not only functional in usage but easy to handle because of its **164.** _____ wheels.

Starting as an **165.** _____ writer, Ryan set up high standards and goals, took an active attitude, and worked non-stop to become professional in his field.

To Natalie, it has been her lifelong ambition to enter the **166.** _____ business, become a celebrity, and make huge amounts of money.

The senior supervisor commented that there was still much room left to be desired, which showed the **167.** _____ that he wasn't satisfied with the results and we'd better work harder.

Due to drunk driving and breaking the speed limit, the driver was brought to the police station for serious traffic **168.** _____.

A	shiftable	**B**	transparent	**C**	thrifty
D	amateur	**E**	unified	**F**	adaptable
G	entertainment	**H**	standardized	**I**	measurement
J	transportation	**K**	uncultured	**L**	prolific
M	violation	**N**	uniformed	**O**	adjustable
P	excessive	**Q**	implication	**R**	economical
S	audible	**T**	automation	**U**	mechanization
V	equivalent	**W**	estimated	**X**	synonymous

Unit 1 石頭人：惡劣環境中的優秀學生

Benjamin Jacob Grimm was born on Yancy Street, a tough **1.** _____ in the Lower East Side of New York City. Due to a family **2.** _____, Ben was raised by his uncle Jake. Ben found a way to **3.** _____ in the neighborhood and once led the Yancy Street gang. Even though he was raised in a bad area, he did very well in **4.** _____ in high school. Thus, he **5.** _____ a full scholarship to Empire State University. He met his **6.** _____ friend, Reed Richards, who was basically a **7.** _____. When they were in school, Reed often told Ben that his dream was to build a space rocket to **8.** _____ the regions of space around Mars. After earning his degree in **9.** _____, Ben joined the United States Marine Corps and became a test **10.** _____. Later on, he joined the Air Force. He was ordered to serve as a pilot during a top-secret **11.** _____ mission into Vladivostok in the Soviet Union. His **12.** _____ were Logan, who became Wolverine, and Carol Danvers, who became Ms. Marvel in the future. After that, he became an **13.** _____ for NASA.

Years later, Reed actually built the spaceship. However, the government denied his **14.** _____ to fly the spaceship by himself. Therefore, he **15.** _____ Ben and asked Ben to fly with him in secrecy. Ben was **16.** _____ to fly the spaceship, but eventually gave in.

A	genius	**B**	football
C	explore	**D**	neighborhood
E	surveillance	**F**	partners
G	permission	**H**	tragedy
I	received	**J**	engineering
K	contacted	**L**	survive
M	lifelong	**N**	astronaut
O	reluctant	**P**	pilot

　　班傑明‧雅各‧格林出生於紐約下東城附近很難生存的楊希街。由於家庭悲劇，班是由他的叔叔傑克所帶大的。班發現他在鄰里中生存的方式，曾經一度領導楊希街的幫派。雖然他是在一個壞區長大，他在高中時的足球成績很好，因此，他獲得了全額獎學金進入了帝國州立大學。他遇到了他一生的朋友，一位天才，里德‧李查茲。當他們在學校時，里德經常告訴班，他的夢想是建立一個太空火箭，探索火星周圍的空間區域。得到他的工程學位後，班加入了美國海軍陸戰隊，成為一名試飛員。後來，他加入了空軍。他奉命在蘇聯符拉迪沃斯托克的秘密任務中作為飛行員。他的合作夥伴是洛根，最終成為金剛狼，和卡羅‧丹佛斯，未來成為驚奇女士。在此之後，他成為了美國宇航局的宇航員。

　　多年以後，里德竟然建成了太空船。然而，政府否決了他自己飛行太空船的許可。因此，他聯繫班，並要求班與他秘密飛行。班原本是不願飛太空船的，但最終同意。

▶▶ 參考答案

1.	D	2.	H
3.	L	4.	B
5.	I	6.	M
7.	A	8.	C
9.	J	10.	P
11.	E	12.	F
13.	N	14.	G
15.	K	16.	O

Part 1 同義字模擬試題

Part 2 填空題模擬試題

Part 3 聽、讀整合能力強化

Unit 2 石頭人：輻射造成石頭人的誕生

Reed, and his wife Susan Storm, her brother Johnny Storm and Ben took the **1.** _____ ride into the upper **2.** _____ of Earth and the Van Allen Belts. Right at that moment, their spaceship was **3.** _____ by a cosmic ray storm and exposed to **4.** _____. The spaceship crashed down to Earth. Luckily, no one was killed. Instead, all four of them found out that they had gained **5.** _____ powers. Ben's skin got transformed into a thick, **6.** _____ orange hide. He became The Thing. Ben was unhappy with his transformation, but still decided to use his superpower to help **7.** _____. He did try many ways to transform back to his human form, but his body **8.** _____ all the attempts. He eventually accepted the fact that he will forever be The Thing.

As his body is **9.** _____ with an orange, flexible, rock-like skin, the Thing is capable of **10.** _____ impacts of great strength and force. He can also **11.** _____ gunfire. He does get injured and he does **12.** _____, but you can never **13.** _____ hurt him. Not only externally, the Thing's senses can withstand higher levels of sensory **14.** _____ than those of a regular human being, except the sense of touch due to his thick skin. And even though he only has three fingers and a thumb on each hand after transforming into the Thing, his actions are not **15.** _____ by this a bit. He remains a great fighter and a **16.** _____ pilot.

A	superhuman	**B**	seriously
C	bleed	**D**	humanity
E	pelted	**F**	surviving
G	skilled	**H**	lumpy
I	radiation	**J**	withstand
K	affected	**L**	atmosphere
M	unauthorized	**N**	covered
O	stimulation	**P**	rejected

Part 1 同義字模擬試題

Part 2 填空題模擬試題

Part 3 聽、讀整合能力強化

▶▶ 中譯

　　里德和他的妻子蘇珊史東，她的弟弟強尼史東和班擅自開往大氣層上層的艾倫輻射帶。就在那一刻，他們的太空飛船被宇宙射線風暴攻擊並暴露在輻射中。飛船墜毀。幸運的是，沒有人死亡。反而，他們四個發現，他們都獲得了超能力。班的皮膚變成厚厚的、詭異的橙色皮。他變成石頭人。班不滿他的轉變，但還是決定用自己的超能力幫助人類。他也嘗試了很多方法來改造回到他的人形，但他的身體拒絕了所有的嘗試。他最終接受了這個事實，他將永遠成為石頭人。

　　由於他的身體上覆蓋著一層橙色的、靈活的、岩石般的皮膚，石頭人能夠承受強大力量與壓力。他也能承受槍炮。他會受傷也會流血，但你永遠無法嚴重傷害他。不僅在外部，石頭人的厚皮可以感受到比一般人更纖細的感官刺激，除了觸覺以外。即使他左右各只有三根手指和一個拇指，他的行動並不會受到一點影響。他仍然是一個偉大的戰士和一個熟練的飛行員。

▶▶ 參考答案

1.	M	2.	L
3.	E	4.	I
5.	A	6.	H
7.	D	8.	P
9.	N	10.	F
11.	J	12.	C
13.	B	14.	O
15.	K	16.	G

Part 1 同義字模擬試題

Part 2 填空題模擬試題

Part 3 聽、讀整合能力強化

Unit 3 末日博士：多變的際遇促成西藏之旅

Victor is not so much an **1.** _____ of the Thing as the enemy of the Fantastic Four. Victor von Doom was born in a small **2.** _____ country named Latveria. His parents are Werner, a doctor and Cynthia von Doom, a witch who had **3.** _____ the demon Mephisto for power. His parents died when he was young, leaving him to Werner's best friend, Boris, to take care of Victor. When Victor found out about his mother's **4.** _____ artifacts, he started to learn **5.** _____ by himself, hoping to set his mother's **6.** _____ free. After graduating from **7.** _____ school, he became a scientific **8.** _____. His works were somehow seen by the American Academies. He was invited to the New York's Empire State University on a full scholarship. After checking himself into the university, Victor was **9.** _____ to the same room as Reed Richards, but somehow Victor just didn't like the **10.** _____. He refused to share a room with Reed and rejected to be **11.** _____ with him. Throughout his university days, Victor pursed a **12.** _____ with Reed.

To rescue his mother's soul from the **13.** _____, he spent a lot of time inventing a machine, but **14.** _____ in his work not only caused a huge explosion, but also ruined his **15.** _____ and get him expelled from school. He decided to leave the States and went to Tibet to seek new **16.** _____.

A	netherworld	**B**	genius
C	invoked	**D**	soul
E	appearance	**F**	enemy
G	arrangement	**H**	assigned
I	mystical	**J**	sorcery
K	rivalry	**L**	friends
M	elementary	**N**	European
O	enlightenment	**P**	miscalculation

Part 1 同義字模擬試題

Part 2 填空題模擬試題

Part 3 聽、讀整合能力強化

▶▶ 中譯

　　與其說維克多是石頭人的一個敵人，可能更適合說，他是驚奇 **4**
超人的敵人。維克多·馮·杜姆出生在一個名為拉托維尼亞的小小歐
洲國家。他的父母是沃納（一名醫生）和辛西婭·馮·杜姆（一個向
惡魔墨菲斯托請求能力的巫婆）。他父母於他年輕時就過世，把他留
給沃納最好的朋友鮑里斯來照顧維克多。當維克多發現了他母親的神
秘文物，他開始自己學習巫術，希望可以解放他母親的靈魂。小學畢
業後，他成為了一個科學天才。他的作品在某種程度上被美國科學院
看到。他被邀請以全額獎學金的方式到紐約帝國州立大學就讀。報到
入學後，維克多被分配到與里德·李查茲同一個房間，但不知為何維
克多就是不喜歡這個安排。他拒絕與里德分一個房間，並拒絕與他交
朋友。在他的大學時代，維克多多次與里德較勁。

　　為了從陰間拯救他媽媽的靈魂，他花許多時間發明機器。但是計
算失誤不只導致巨大的爆炸，更使得他毀容跟遭學校開除。他決定離
開美國，去西藏尋求新的啟示。

▶▶ 參考答案

1. F		2. N	
3. C		4. I	
5. J		6. D	
7. M		8. B	
9. H		10. G	
11. L		12. K	
13. A		14. P	
15. E		16. O	

He found the Aged Geng his and a long-lost order of **1. _____**. The monks made the first suit of **2. _____** which hid his features from the world. The mask was also put on him before it was **3. _____**. Victor went back to his homeland Latveria, using his genius and **4. _____** to transform it into the Doom Utopia. Victor set up three **5. _____**: to rescue his mother's soul, to be better than Reed Richards, and to conquer the world. Dr. Doom began an **6. _____** with several different villains, such as the Sub-Mariner and alien Ovoids to **7. _____** new powers and to take down the Fantastic Four, but he was always so close to **8. _____**.

Dr. Doom never gave up. He then engaged Reed in a **9. _____** battle at the Latverian Embassy. Doom used an encephalo-gun and thought he had **10. _____** Reed into Limbo. However, in reality, Reed had **11. _____** Doom instead. When Doom came back from the **12. _____**, he again attacked the Fantastic Four. The Thing was furious and crushed Doom's hands inside his **13. _____** and allowed him to **14. _____** away. Doom would never forget the **15. _____** and swore he would come back for **16. _____**.

A	mental	**B**	revenge
C	alliance	**D**	monks
E	mesmerism	**F**	hypnotized
G	goals	**H**	armor
I	cooled	**J**	technology
K	slink	**L**	gauntlets
M	gain	**N**	casted
O	humiliation	**P**	success

　　他發現了老年的成吉思汗和久違的僧侶。僧侶們做第一套兵器，讓他可以在世界中隱藏他的真實身份。面具也在冷卻前被戴上。維克多又回到了他的祖國拉托維尼亞，用他的天才和技術，將拉脫維尼亞改造為杜姆式的烏托邦。維克多設立了三個目標：拯救他母親的靈魂，比里德·李查茲出色，征服世界。末日博士則與幾個不同的惡棍結盟，如潛水俠和外來卵形體以獲得新的力量來打倒驚奇 4 超人，但他卻總是那麼接近成功。

　　末日博士從來沒有放棄過。爾後，他在拉托維尼亞大使館裡與里德開始了一場腦力的戰鬥。末日博士使用 encephalo 槍，以為他已經成功地將里德推向地獄邊境。然而， 在現實中，里德卻催眠了末日博士。當末日博士從催眠中醒來後，他再次攻擊驚奇 4 超人。石頭人大怒，粉碎了末日博士在手套內的手，但允許他偷偷溜走。末日博士永遠也不會忘記這個屈辱，發誓他會回來報仇。

▶▶ 參考答案

1.	D	2.	H
3.	I	4.	J
5.	G	6.	C
7.	M	8.	P
9.	A	10.	N
11.	F	12.	E
13.	L	14.	K
15.	O	16.	B

Unit 5 快銀：加入復仇者成為英雄隊

A gypsy couple, Django and Marya Miximoff have a twin brother and sister named Pietro and Wanda. Both of them **1.** _____ that they had **2.** _____ talents when they were teenagers. One day, their gypsy **3.** _____ was attacked by **4.** _____. Pietro used his phenomenal **5.** _____ and fled from the camp with his sister. Wanda and Pietro had nowhere to go. They **6.** _____ central Europe and living off the land. One day, Wanda accidentally used her **7.** _____ hex powers and set a house on fire. They were chased away by the townspeople. Right before they were about to get caught, they were **8.** _____ by Magneto who is their **9.** _____ father. This **10.** _____ was never revealed until they were both grown up.

Magneto isn't a good **11.** _____, either. He owns the Brotherhood of Evil Mutants and made the twins become members of it as Quicksilver and the Scarlet Witch. For months, they **12.** _____ in the Brotherhood until the **13.** _____ Stranger **14.** _____ Magneto from earth. They left the Brotherhood right away and **15.** _____ the Avengers to become part of the hero team **16.** _____ Captain America and Hawkeye.

A	wandered	**B**	fellow
C	secret	**D**	served
E	biological	**F**	extraterrestrial
G	peculiar	**H**	camp
I	alongside	**J**	villagers
K	transported	**L**	speed
M	discovered	**N**	uncontrollable
O	joined	**P**	rescued

▶▶ 中譯

　　一對吉普賽夫婦，狄亞哥和瑪麗亞梅西摩夫有對孿生兄妹名為琵也達和萬達。他們在青少年時就發現了他們有特殊的才能。有一天，他們的吉普賽營地遭到村民襲擊。琵也達用他驚人的速度與他的妹妹從營中逃出。萬達和琵也達無處可去。他們漫步歐洲中部，靠土地為生。有一天，無意中萬達用了她不可控制的魔法力量，引發房子著火。他們被市民追逐。在他們即將陷入對方手裡之前，他們被自己的親生父親萬磁王救出。這個秘密從未被揭露，直到他們長大。

　　萬磁王也不是一個好人。他擁有邪惡的突變兄弟會，並將這對雙胞胎變為其中成員，將他們命名為快銀與猩紅巫婆。幾個月來，他們兄妹都在為兄弟會服務，直到萬磁王被陌生人從地球上帶走。他們離開了兄弟會並馬上加入了復仇者，成為英雄隊，並跟隨美國隊長和鷹眼。

▶▶ 參考答案

1.	M	2.	G
3.	H	4.	J
5.	L	6.	A
7.	N	8.	P
9.	E	10.	C
11.	B	12.	D
13.	F	14.	K
15.	O	16.	I

Part 1 同義字模擬試題

Part 2 填空題模擬試題

Part 3 聽、讀整合能力強化

Unit 6　快銀：修補裂痕、從幫派到超級英雄

Wanda had been close to her brother until she started to date the Vision. Pietro did not agree with the **1.** _____ because the Vision is inhuman and caused their first **2.** _____. Later on, Pietro actually married his **3.** _____, Crystal who is also an inhuman. Pietro and Wanda eventually **4.** _____ their rift.

Quicksilver has an **5.** _____ personality. He once joined the U.S. government-sponsored X-Factor team. He told the **6.** _____ how **7.** _____ he was at dealing with a world where almost everyone and everything is slow and even **8.** _____. Quicksilver can not only run at a **9.** _____ speed, but also has a fast **10.** _____ so that he can recover from his wounds faster than an **11.** _____ human being. Because of his speed, he can create cyclone-strength **12.** _____, run up walls and cross bodies of water. Quicksilver once lost his power of speed. Fortunately, Terrigen Mist, an inhuman, gave him some new powers. Quicksilver is able to **13.** _____ himself out of mainstream time and space and go into the future. Although he **14.** _____ his new power well, he still desired to get his former powers back, but he had no clue how to do so. It was not until one time that he felt a desire to help a woman in **15.** _____ danger did he **16.** _____ his power back. He saved the woman's life after all.

A	performed	**B**	stupid
C	relationship	**D**	psychologist
E	displace	**F**	rift
G	frustrated	**H**	impatient
I	regain	**J**	rescuer
K	supersonic	**L**	mended
M	mortal	**N**	metabolism
O	ordinary	**P**	winds

▶▶ 中譯

萬達一直都與她的哥哥很親近,直到她開始與幻視約會。因為幻視並非人類,琵也達不認同他們的關係。這件事造成他們兄妹之間的第一個裂痕。後來,琵也達娶了他的救命恩人水晶,水晶居然也是非人類。琵也達與萬達最終修補他們之間的裂痕。

快銀有不耐煩的個性。他曾經參加了美國政府資助的 X 因素隊伍。他告訴心理學家,他在一個幾乎每個人,一切都是緩慢的,甚至愚蠢的的世界裡是多痛苦的一件事。快銀不只能以超音速的速度運行,他也有一個快速的新陳代謝,使他的傷口可以比普通人更快地恢復。因為他的速度,他可以創造颶風強度的大風,跑上牆壁和跑過水面。快銀曾經一度失去了他的速度。幸運的是,泰勒‧霧,一位非人類,給了他一些新的力量。快銀能夠將自己擺脫主流的時間和空間到未來。雖然他很會執行他新的力量,但仍然希望能夠恢復他以前的力量,但他不知道如何做到這一點。直到有一次感到需要幫助一個生命遭遇危險的女人,他才重獲他的力量。他最終拯救了這位婦女的生命。

▶▶ 參考答案

1. C	2. F
3. J	4. L
5. H	6. D
7. G	8. B
9. K	10. N
11. O	12. P
13. E	14. A
15. M	16. I

Unit 7 萬磁王：加入復仇者成為英雄隊

Born into a **1.** _____ family in the late 1920s, Magneto and his family were faced with **2.** _____ and hardship during the Nazi reign. His family escaped to Poland but were still **3.** _____ by the Germans. They were later sent to the Warsaw Ghetto attempting to escape again but failed. Instead, his mother and sister were **4.** _____. Magneto on the other hand survived probably because the Germans saw his **5.** _____ powers. He was sent to Auschwitz, where he met his wife Magda. The couple moved to the Ukrainian city of Vinnytsia. They had a daughter named Anya. One day, a group of angry **6.** _____ showed up which caused Magneto to **7.** _____ his power and accidentally burned down the house with Anya still inside. Magda was **8.** _____ by his **9.** _____ behavior and power and left him.

Since then, Magneto never tried to hide his power and his **10.** _____. He was **11.** _____ to be a mutant. In fact, he is willing to use the deadly force to **12.** _____ mutants. He believes that mutants will eventually be a **13.** _____ lifeform and will take over the **14.** _____. Humankind will enter into **15.** _____. He has no **16.** _____ to live peacefully with other kinds.

A	world	**B**	irrational
C	mob	**D**	intentions
E	dominant	**F**	captured
G	Jewish	**H**	discrimination
I	identity	**J**	proud
K	protect	**L**	executed
M	appalled	**N**	unleash
O	slavery	**P**	mutant

Part 1 同義字模擬試題

Part 2 填空題模擬試題

Part 3 聽、讀整合能力強化

▶▶ 中譯

在 20 年代末期，出生於一個猶太家庭，萬磁王和他的家人在納粹掌權期間面臨歧視和苦難。他的家人逃到波蘭，但仍然被德國人所捕獲。他們後來被送到華沙猶太區，試圖再次逃跑，但沒有成功。他的母親和妹妹反而被處決。萬磁王卻倖存下來，因為德國人看到了他突變體的力量。他被送往奧斯威辛集中營，在那裡他遇到了他的妻子瑪格達。這對夫婦搬到了烏克蘭的文尼斯。他們有一個叫安雅的女兒。有一天，一群憤怒的暴徒出現了，造成萬磁王釋放他的力量並意外燒毀房子，而安雅還在裡面。瑪格達被他的不合乎常理的行為嚇到而離開他。

此後，萬磁王就沒有試圖掩蓋他的能力和他的身份。他很自豪身為一個突變體。事實上，他更願意利用致命的武力來保護突變體。他認為，突變體最終會取代人類，佔主導地位，接管世界。人類將成為奴隸。他無意與其他生物和平共存。

▶▶ 參考答案

1.	G	2.	H
3.	F	4.	L
5.	P	6.	C
7.	N	8.	M
9.	B	10.	I
11.	J	12.	K
13.	E	14.	A
15.	O	16.	D

Part 1 同義字模擬試題

Part 2 填空題模擬試題

Part 3 聽、讀整合能力強化

Unit 8 萬磁王：打回原形、重組了邪惡兄弟會

To him, it's Mutant kind or nobody. With the power to control all forms of **1.** _____, Magneto is able to **2.** _____ magnetic fields. He can also use his power in several different **3.** _____ at once. He can also project any types of energy that are part of the electromagnetic **4.** _____ such as radio waves, ultralights, and x-rays, and furthermore manipulate them. He does have a **5.** _____ though. His body doesn't self-heal, and his power is **6.** _____ upon his **7.** _____ condition. It means that after injury, his body is unable to **8.** _____ the strain of manipulating great amounts of **9.** _____ forces. In fact, he becomes a normal human being.

Magneto's first **10.** _____ act is attacking a U.S military base called Cape Citadel. He was driven off by the X-Men. He then gathered a group of **11.** _____ mutants who were full of anger and formed the Brotherhood of Evil. His kids, Quicksilver and Scarlet Witch were forced to be a part of the group as well. Although by then, neither of them knew they were **12.** _____ related. Magneto tried to **13.** _____ a mutant homeland in the South but again was **14.** _____ by the X-Men. Magneto was then captured by the Stranger and was sent to another planet. During that period of time, the Brotherhood fell apart. Quicksilver, Scarlet Witch and the other mutants **15.** _____ him. Magneto found his way to escape to Earth and **16.** _____ the Brotherhood of Evil. His goal remains the same —Mutants will conquer the world!

A	deserted	**B**	locations
C	establish	**D**	biologically
E	spectrum	**F**	weakness
G	foiled	**H**	dependent
I	reassembled	**J**	magnetic
K	withstand	**L**	manipulate
M	magnetism	**N**	physical
O	villainous	**P**	disillusioned

Part 1 同義字模擬試題

Part 2 填空題模擬試題

Part 3 聽、讀整合能力強化

對他來說，這是突變體的天下。擁有能控制各種形式的磁的力量，萬磁王能夠操縱磁場。他可以同時在不同的地區使用他的力量，也可以投射一部份任何類型電磁頻譜的能量，如無線電波、超輕型和X射線，進一步操縱它們。他確實有弱點。他的身體不會自癒，他的力量取決於他的身體狀況。這意味著，受傷後，他的身體是無法承受操縱大量磁力的應變。事實上，他將成為一般人。

萬磁王的第一個惡棍行為是攻擊在海角城堡的一個美軍基地。他被X戰警趕走。然後，他聚集了一批失望且充滿憤怒的突變，並創造了邪惡兄弟會。他的孩子，快銀和猩紅巫婆也被迫成為集團的一部分。雖然在當時，他們不知道他們是有血緣關係的。萬磁王試圖在南方建立一個突變體的家園，但再次被X戰警挫敗。萬磁王之後被陌生人捕獲，並送往另一個星球。那段時間，兄弟會土崩瓦解。快銀、猩紅巫婆和其他突變體拋棄了他。萬磁王找到了自己掙脫的方式回到地球，並重組了邪惡兄弟會。他的目標仍然是相同的突變體征服世界！

▶▶ 參考答案

1. M	2. L
3. B	4. E
5. F	6. H
7. N	8. K
9. J	10. O
11. P	12. D
13. C	14. G
15. A	16. I

Part 1 同義字模擬試題

Part 2 填空題模擬試題

Part 3 聽、讀整合能力強化

Unit 9 忍者龜：普林斯特和四隻烏龜

The story of the Teenage Mutant Ninja Turtles, **1.** _____ as TMNT, starts with a rat in Japan. Hamato Yoshi, who was great at Ninjitsu owned a **2.** _____ rat named Splinter. Splinter liked to **3.** _____ Yoshi when he practiced his Ninjitsu. One day , Yoshi accidentally killed his **4.** _____ named Oroku Nagi during a fight. He then took Splinter and **5.** _____ to the U.S.A. Nagi's brother eventually **6.** _____ him down and killed him, leaving Splinter on the street. Until one day, he saw a road **7.** _____ involving a truck carrying **8.** _____ waste.

Four turtles fell out of the truck into a **9.** _____. Splinter followed them down and saw the four turtles covered in the **10.** _____. He tried to help them and ended up with ooze all over himself too. The next day, not knowing **11.** _____ why, the five of them all had **12.** _____ in size and intellect. They all began walking **13.** _____ and started to speak as human beings. Splinter named the 4 turtles after four **14.** _____ Italian artists. Knowing the **15.** _____ world would not understand them, the five of them made their home **16.** _____ of New York City.

A	exactly	**B**	doubled
C	outside	**D**	mimic
E	shortened	**F**	manhole
G	accident	**H**	pet
I	sewers	**J**	rival
K	immigrated	**L**	ooze
M	Renaissance	**N**	toxic
O	upright	**P**	tracked

Part 1 同義字模擬試題

Part 2 填空題模擬試題

Part 3 聽、讀整合能力強化

▶▶ 中譯

關於忍者龜的故事，縮寫為 TMNT，始於日本的一隻老鼠。Hamato Yoshi 擅長忍術，他擁有一隻寵物鼠名為普林斯特。斯普林特最喜歡在他的主人練習忍術時模仿他。有一次，Yoshi 在一次對戰中不慎殺死了他的對手 Oroku Nagi。隨後，他便與斯普林特移民到美國，Nagi 的弟弟最終找到了他，並將他殺死。使得斯普林特流落街頭。直到有一天，他看到一台運載有毒廢料卡車發生交通事故。

四隻烏龜跌出了卡車進入了下水道。斯普林特跟著他們，只見四隻烏龜被蓋在軟泥之中。他試圖幫助他們，也讓自己滿布軟泥。第二天，不知道為什麼，他們五個的大小和智力都多了一倍。他們都開始直立行走，並開始說人話。斯普林特替四個烏龜依照文藝復興時期的意大利藝術家命名。他們了解外面的世界不會明白他們，因此他們五個生活在紐約市的下水道。

▶▶ 參考答案

1.	E	2.	H
3.	D	4.	J
5.	K	6.	P
7.	G	8.	N
9.	F	10.	L
11.	A	12.	B
13.	O	14.	M
15.	C	16.	I

Unit 10 忍者龜：四隻烏龜，四種性格

The four brothers look **1.** _____ yet are very different. Donatello is the scientist, inventor, engineer, and **2.** _____ genius. He wears a **3.** _____ mask and fights with a Bo. He prefers to use his knowledge to solve **4.** _____ instead of fighting. Leonardo, on the other hand is the tactical, **5.** _____ leader. He wears a blue mask and fights with Katana. He often bears the **6.** _____ of responsibility for his brothers, which commonly leads to conflict with Raphael. Michelangelo is the most **7.** _____ teenager of the team. He is free spirited and goofy. He is also the one that loves **8.** _____ the most. Michelangelo wears an orange mask and fights with a pair of Nunchucks. He also has a Southern Californian **9.** _____. Raphael wears a red mask and fights with a pair of Sai. He is **10.** _____ stronger than other three and much more **11.** _____ as well. He sometimes fights with his brothers, but he is also **12.** _____ loyal to his brothers and sensei.

When the turtles were 13 years old, Splinter thought their training was **13.** _____ and they were ready to face off against the street gang, Purple Dragon. He told them of their origin and told them that he was already too old to battle. He asked the turtles to **14.** _____ the death of his old master. The TMNT successfully took down Saki and the Purple Dragon. They then started to use their skills to battle **15.** _____ and evil overlords while attempting to remain **16.** _____ from society. Interestingly, their favorite food is pizza.

Part 1 同義字模擬試題

Part 2 填空題模擬試題

Part 3 聽、讀整合能力強化

A	physically	**B**	similar
C	complete	**D**	accent
E	purple	**F**	pizza
G	criminals	**H**	technological
I	aggressive	**J**	courageous
K	stereotypical	**L**	conflicts
M	avenge	**N**	intensely
O	hidden	**P**	burden

▶▶ 中譯

　　四個兄弟看似雷同，但卻有很大的不同。多納泰羅是科學家、發明家、工程師和技術天才。他戴著紫色面具並用棒子攻擊。他喜歡用自己的知識來解決衝突，而不是戰鬥。李奧納多則是戰略性、勇敢的領導人。他戴著一件藍色的面具，用武士刀攻擊。他經常為他的兄弟承擔一切，這通常是導致他與拉斐爾發生衝突的原因。米開朗基羅是典型的青少年。他崇尚精神自由和滑稽。他也是最愛永存於人們心中的英雄霸主吃比薩餅的一位。米開朗基羅戴橘色面具並用雙截棍攻擊。他也有一個南加州的口音。拉斐爾則是戴著紅色面具和用一對刀劍攻擊。他身體比其他三個都強壯，也更加積極好鬥。他有時與他的兄弟打架，但他也強烈地忠於自己的兄弟和老師。

　　當烏龜們 13 歲時，斯普林特認為他們的培訓已經完成，並已準備好面對反派的街頭幫派，紫金神龍。他告訴他們，他們的原生並表示他已經太老無法戰鬥。他要求烏龜們替他的老主人報復。忍者龜成功的拿下 Sak i 和紫金神龍。然後，他們就開始用他們的能力戰鬥罪犯和邪惡的統治者，並試圖躲藏在社會之中。有趣的是，他們最喜歡的食物是披薩。

▶▶ 參考答案

1.	B	2.	H
3.	E	4.	L
5.	J	6.	P
7.	K	8.	F
9.	D	10.	A
11.	I	12.	N
13.	C	14.	M
15.	G	16.	O

Unit 11 許瑞德：與四隻烏龜的生死鬥

Oroku Saki is a normal human with great strength, **1.** _____, and agility. He is a great martial arts fighter and brilliant with **2.** _____ in a wide variety of sciences. When he was a little boy, his **3.** _____ older brother Oroku Nagi was killed by Hamato Toshi in a battle for a woman Tang Shen. Saki swore the revenge and **4.** _____ in the Foot Clan. He soon rose up the ranks and became their most **5.** _____ warrior. He was also chosen to lead the American **6.** _____ of the Foot in New York at the age of 18. Although he was still very young, he **7.** _____ the identity of the Shredder and **8.** _____ both Yoshi and Shen. His cold heart made him very successful in the **9.** _____ circle of New York. He basically built the **10.** _____ criminal empire which was involved in drug **11.** _____, arms running, and assassinations. One day, when he was doing some **12.** _____ business, a sai blade came through the window with a **13.** _____ on it. The note said that someone wanted to challenge Shredder to a **14.** _____ to the death. Shredder of course showed up at the **15.** _____, but surprisingly, he saw 4 giant turtles **16.** _____ for him.

A	note	**B**	enrolled
C	criminal	**D**	battle
E	respectful	**F**	duel
G	stamina	**H**	formidable
I	waiting	**J**	branch
K	shady	**L**	murdered
M	skilled	**N**	adopted
O	smuggling	**P**	aptitudes

▶▶ 中譯

Oroku Saki 是一個普通人類，但具有巨大的力量，耐力和敏捷性。他是一個很好的武術高手，也在各種科學性向上都很聰明。當他還是一個小男孩時，他敬愛的哥哥 Oroku Yoshi 在一場為一個名為唐軒的女人的戰鬥中被 Hamato Yoshiko 殺死。Saki 發誓報復，並報名參加了腳族。他很快的在排名中名列前茅，並成為他們最熟練的戰士。他也被選為領導在紐約腳族的美國分支時，只有 18 歲。雖然他還很年輕，他採用了許瑞德這個身份，並謀殺了 Yoshi 與唐軒。他的冷血，使他在紐約的犯罪圈裡非常的成功。他基本上建立了強大的犯罪帝國，並參與毒品走私、軍火運行和暗殺。有一天，當他在做一些見不得人的事業時，一個帶有字條的刀從窗口飛進來。這個字條說明了有人想挑戰許瑞德，決鬥到死。許瑞德當然出現在戰鬥的地點，但令人驚訝的，他看到的是四隻巨型烏龜在等著他。

▶▶ 參考答案

1.	G	2.	P
3.	E	4.	B
5.	M	6.	J
7.	N	8.	L
9.	C	10.	H
11.	O	12.	K
13.	A	14.	F
15.	D	16.	I

Unit 12 許瑞德：被炸成碎片後又復活出現

The turtles took down the Foot Ninjas and Shredder decided to take on the turtles by himself. Shredder was indeed very **1.** _____ at martial arts. The four needed to **2.** _____ him together in order to get a chance to **3.** _____. At the end, Leonardo scored a lucky shot by **4.** _____ his sword through the Shredder's **5.** _____. As a ninja, Shredder would not want to live with **6.** _____. He asked them to "finish it", but Leonardo told him to take down his own life. Shredder **7.** _____ that if he must take his own life, he will take the turtles lives with him. He took out a Thermite Bomb which would wipe the **8.** _____ clean of all life. Donatello quickly used his Bo to knock Shredder and the **9.** _____ off the roof. As he fell the bomb exploded and tore Shredder to pieces.

Almost a year after, on **10.** _____ eve, Leonardo went out for a training and was attacked by a literal army of Foot Soldiers. Leonardo was badly **11.** _____ and crashed through the window while going home. He told the rest of the team, the Shredder is back. The Foot Clan soon came bursting into the house and an **12.** _____ battle started. Unexpectedly, Raphael's friend Casey Jones showed up and battled Shredder **13.** _____. The building caught on **14.** _____, and before the police and the fire trucks **15.** _____, Shredder ordered his people to **16.** _____, but he promised he would come back.

A	rooftop	**B**	injured
C	plunging	**D**	battle
E	approached	**F**	torso
G	bomb	**H**	succeed
I	intense	**J**	shame
K	Christmas	**L**	directly
M	good	**N**	responded
O	fire	**P**	retreat

▶▶ 中譯

　　烏龜們拿下了腳族忍者。許瑞德決定自己對付烏龜。許瑞德確實非常好武。四隻烏龜需要一起對戰他，才會有成功的機會。最後，李奧納多幸運地一劍插進許瑞德的軀幹裡。作為一個忍者，許瑞德不想忍辱偷生。他要他們「結束它」，但李奧納多要他自己結束自己的生命。許瑞德回應，如果他必須結束自己的生命，他也會一起結束烏龜們的生命。他拿出一個可以結束屋頂下所有生命的鋁熱劑炸彈。多納泰羅迅速地用自己的棍棒將許瑞德和炸彈打往半空中。當他落下時，炸彈爆炸，將許瑞德炸成碎片。

　　將近一年後的聖誕節，李奧納多出外訓練時被腳族的軍隊攻擊。李奧納多受到重傷，並溜過窗口趕回家。他告訴其他人，許瑞德又回來了。腳族很快就衝進了屋子，激烈的戰鬥開始了。沒想到，拉斐爾的朋友凱西・瓊斯出現了，直接與許瑞德開始交戰。建築物開始著火，警察和消防車到之前，許瑞德命令他的人撤退。但是他承諾，他會再回來。

▶▶ 參考答案

1.	M	2.	D
3.	H	4.	C
5.	F	6.	J
7.	N	8.	A
9.	G	10.	K
11.	B	12.	I
13.	L	14.	O
15.	E	16.	P

Unit 13　金鋼狼：狼爪的發現、再生能力

The son of rich **1.** _____ owners John and Elizabeth Howlett, James Howlett was born in Cold Lake, Alberta, Canada. One day, James happened to see an **2.** _____ that the groundkeeper, Thomas Logan killed John Howlett. It was the first time James' claws **3.** _____ from the backs of his hands and he attacked the **4.** _____ with uncharacteristic **5.** _____. He killed Thomas Logan, and scarring Dog's face with three claw marks. James later on **6.** _____ the name "Logan" to hide his **7.** _____. Logan and his childhood **8.** _____, Rose eventually fell in love. However, during an incident while Dog, the son of Thomas Logan was battling with Logan, he **9.** _____ killed Rose with his claws. He had no choice but to leave the **10.** _____ and live in the wilderness among real wolves. Logan is a mutant. He has his **11.** _____ wolf claws and possesses animal-keen sense, **12.** _____ physical capabilities, and powerful **13.** _____ ability known as a healing factor.

While he was a member of Team X, he was given a false memory **14.** _____. It was not until he joined the Canadian Defense Ministry did, he break free of the **15.** _____ control. He then started to work as an intelligence **16.** _____ for the Canadian government and became the first Canadian superhero, Wolverine.

A ferocity

B adopted

C accidentally

D extended

E enhanced

F farm

G identity

H intruders

I regenerative

J playmate

K signature

L incident

M implant

N mental

O operative

P colony

▶▶ 中譯

　　富有農場主人約翰和伊麗莎白·豪利特的兒子，詹姆斯·豪利特出生在加拿大阿爾伯塔省的冷湖。詹姆斯碰巧看到場地管理人，湯瑪斯·洛根殺害約翰·豪利。這是第一次，詹姆斯的爪子從他的手背延伸，他異常兇猛的攻擊入侵者。他殺死了湯瑪斯·洛根，並在道格的臉上留下三個爪痕。詹姆斯後來就採用了「洛根」這個名字，以隱藏自己的身份。洛根和他的童年玩伴羅絲最終墜入愛河。然而，在湯瑪斯·洛根的兒子道格與洛根對戰時，意外發生了，他的爪子偶然地殺害了羅絲。他只好離開群體，生活在真正荒野的狼群中。洛根是一個突變體。他有著他著名的狼爪，擁有動物敏銳的感覺，進階的體能，和稱為癒合因子強大的再生能力。

　　爾後，他在軍隊裡被植入了假的記憶體。直到他加入加拿大國防部才掙脫了精神控制。然後，他開始作為一個情報人員並和加拿大政府合作，成為加拿大的第一位超級英雄，金剛狼。

▶▶ 參考答案

1. F	2. L
3. D	4. H
5. A	6. B
7. G	8. J
9. C	10. P
11. K	12. E
13. I	14. M
15. N	16. O

Unit 14 金鋼狼：救兒子達肯、被硬化的亞德曼金屬所殺死

Wolverine was later on **1.** _____ by Professor Charles Xavier to the superhero mutant team, the X-Men. One time, it was not until that the supervillain Magneto **2.** _____ the adamantium from Wolverine's **3.** _____ did he first realize that his claws are actually bone. It took him a long time to heal from the **4.** _____ trauma which caused his healing factor to burn out. Wolverine returned back to the X-Men. Once, the villain Apocalypse caught Wolverine, and **5.** _____ him into becoming the Horseman Death. Wolverine **6.** _____ the programming and returned back to the X-Men. He then joined the Avengers. Wolverine finally **7.** _____ he had a son named Daken. By then, Daken was brainwashed and was working for the **8.** _____ Romulus. Wolverine made it his **9.** _____ to rescue his son and stop Romulus from harming anyone else any more.

In 2014, there was a **10.** _____ from the microverse, which can turndown Wolverine's healing factor and his **11.** _____ will be able to kill him. Other Superhero's, such as Mister Fantastic offered to work on finding a means of **12.** _____ his healing **13.** _____. However, before the **14.** _____ was found, Wolverine was killed by the **15.** _____ Adamantium. The X -Men and the team were **16.** _____ over what happened to Wolverine.

A	solution	**B**	mission
C	massive	**D**	virus
E	discovered	**F**	reactivating
G	overcame	**H**	villain
I	factor	**J**	brainwashed
K	skeleton	**L**	enemies
M	hardening	**N**	removed
O	recruited	**P**	heartbroken

金剛狼後來被查爾斯·澤維爾教授招募到超級英雄突變隊，X 戰警。有一次，在萬磁王去除了金剛狼骨骼裡的亞德曼金屬，金剛狼才第一次意識到，他的爪子實際上是骨頭。因為大面積的創傷，他花了很長的時間癒合傷口。金剛狼回到 X 戰警隊。另一次，千年老妖抓到了金剛狼，企圖將他洗腦，說服他成為死亡騎士。金剛狼克服了編程，並返回 X 戰警隊。之後，他加入了復仇者。金剛狼終於發現他有一個叫達肯的兒子。屆時，達肯已被洗腦，並努力為惡棍羅穆盧斯工作。金剛狼設立了他的使命，他要拯救他的兒子和阻止羅慕盧斯傷害其他任何人。

2014 年，微細病毒可以取消金剛狼的癒合因子，他的敵人就可以殺死他。其他超級英雄的，如奇幻人開始尋找讓癒合因子復活的方式。但是在發現該溶液之前，金剛狼已經被硬化的亞德曼金屬所殺死。X 戰警和團隊對於金剛狼所發生的事傷透了心。

▶▶ 參考答案

1. O	2. N
3. K	4. C
5. J	6. G
7. E	8. H
9. B	10. D
11. L	12. F
13. I	14. A
15. M	16. P

Unit 15 劍齒虎：殺死父親、老男人和銀狐

When Sabretooth was a little boy, he **1.** _____ killed his brother over a piece of pie. That was the first time the mutation was **2.** _____. His canine teeth grew much larger and sharper **3.** _____ to a big cat, and his finger and toenails turned into 20 **4.** _____ talons. He also got claws which were so sharp that could cut through most types of **5.** _____ and structure. His father was terrified and locked him in a **6.** _____. He also built an **7.** _____ system that would pull out Victor's "devil teeth" in an attempt to **8.** _____ his "demons." Victor was treated as an animal for years until one day, he broke the cellar and killed his father. After leaving his own house, he worked for the **9.** _____ at the age of fifteen. One day, during his work, he was picked on by a **10.** _____ older man. Sabretooth couldn't control himself and **11.** _____ him from crotching his throat with his **12.** _____.

As Wolverine's number 1 **13.** _____, Sabretooth and Wolverine's battles go all the way back to 1912. Sabretooth started to **14.** _____ for a man by the name of Hudson. Hudson ordered him to attack a Blackfoot **15.** _____ where Wolverine was living in. Sabretooth ended up **16.** _____ Wolverine's lover, Silverfox.

A	gutted	**B**	cellar
C	accidentally	**D**	manifested
E	belligerent	**F**	railroad
G	retractable	**H**	akin
I	tribe	**J**	flesh
K	automatic	**L**	purge
M	claws	**N**	enemy
O	work	**P**	murdering

▶▶ 中譯

　　當劍齒虎還是一個小男孩時，他偶然地為了一塊派殺害了他的弟弟。這是第一次他突變的因子顯現出來。他的犬齒變得更大更清晰，類似於一隻大型貓科，他的手指和腳趾甲變成了 20 根可以伸縮的爪子。他還擁有了犀利到可以切過大多數類型的肉和結構的爪子。他的父親嚇壞了，把他鎖在地窖裡。他還建立了一個自動系統來自動拔除維克特的「魔鬼牙齒」，企圖清除他的「心魔。」維克特多年來被視為動物，直到有一天，他衝破了地窖，殺死他的父親。離開自己的房子後，15 歲的他便在鐵路工作。在他工作期間的有一天，他被一個好戰的老男人欺負。劍齒虎無法控制自己，他用他的爪子，將對方從胯下割破到他的喉結。

　　作為金剛狼的第一號敵人，劍齒虎和金剛狼的戰鬥可以一路回溯到 1912 年，當劍齒虎開始為一個名為哈德森的人工作時。哈德森命令他攻擊黑腳部落，當時金剛狼正好生活在其中。劍齒虎最終謀殺金剛狼的愛人，銀狐。

▶▶ 參考答案

1.　C	2.　D
3.　H	4.　G
5.　J	6.　B
7.　K	8.　L
9.　F	10. E
11. A	12. M
13. N	14. O
15. I	16. P

Unit 16 劍齒虎：向獨眼巨人借村正妖刀

Years later, Sabretooth became **1.** _____ with a group which killed Wolverine's wife Itsuand the **2.** _____ of her son. Sabretooth then was **3.** _____ into the Avengers in 1959.A few years later, Sabretooth became a member of Team X with Wolverine and Maverick for a **4.** _____ mission, although it didn't last long. He later on joined the Marauders to **5.** _____ the Morlocks. Once again, Sabretooth battled with Wolverine.

Hating the fact that he couldn't control his **6.** _____ rages, Sabretooth once found a **7.** _____ named Birdy who can help him calm down and control his **8.** _____. The situation was good for some time, until one day his son killed Birdy. Sabretooth lost all his **9.** _____. Professor X tried to help him and kept him in the Mansion. However, he wasn't there for long. Sabretooth fought his way out and **10.** _____ the Hound Program to kill! Time after time, Sabretooth saw Wolverine as his number 1 target. He **11.** _____ around the world to gain more power and strength in order to take Wolverine down. Wolverine thought it was time to put an end to Sabretooth so he asked Cyclops for the Muramasa Blade which can **12.** _____ healing factors. Wolverine chased down the **13.** _____ Sabretooth and sliced off his arm. Even though Sabretooth was **14.** _____ injured, he wouldn't **15.** _____. Wolverine ended up killing him. Later on, Professor X **16.** _____ to Wolverine that Sabretooth was actually his first choice to be a member of the X-men.

A	surrender	**B**	involved
C	telepath	**D**	massacre
E	Russian	**F**	nullify
G	emotion	**H**	abduction
I	rejoined	**J**	traveled
K	control	**L**	recruited
M	rabid	**N**	murderous
O	badly	**P**	revealed

▶▶▶ 中譯

　　多年以後，劍齒虎參與殺害了金剛狼的妻子 Itsu 和她兒子綁架案的一群。劍齒虎在 1959 年被招入復仇者。幾年後，因為一個俄羅斯的任務，劍齒虎和金剛狼、獨行俠一起成為 X 小組的一員，雖然並沒有持續多久。後來，他就加入了掠奪者以屠殺莫洛克人。劍齒虎再度的與金剛狼作戰。

　　厭惡無法控制自己殺氣肆虐的事實，劍齒虎有一次發現了一位會心靈感應的人，名為博蒂，可以幫助他冷靜下來，控制住自己的情緒。情況好轉了一段時間，直到有一天他的兒子殺死了博蒂。劍齒虎失去了所有的控制。教授試圖幫助他，並將他留在官邸。不過，他在那裡待不久。劍齒虎找到他逃出去的方法，並重新加入獵犬計劃來殺人！一次又一次，劍齒虎視金剛狼為他的頭號目標。他周遊世界各地以獲得更多的權力和力量，讓他可以將金剛狼拿下。金剛狼認為這是結束劍齒虎的時候，於是詢問獨眼巨人，向他借了可以剔除癒合能力的「村正妖刀」。金剛狼追到狂熱的劍齒虎並割下他的手臂。儘管劍齒虎受了重傷，他也不投降。金剛狼最終殺害了他。後來，X 教授透露給金剛狼知道，實際上他認為能成為 X 戰警成員的第一選擇其實是劍齒虎。

▶▶ 參考答案

1.	B	2.	H
3.	L	4.	E
5.	D	6.	N
7.	C	8.	G
9.	K	10.	I
11.	J	12.	F
13.	M	14.	O
15.	A	16.	P

Part 1 同義字模擬試題

Part 2 填空題模擬試題

Part 3 聽、讀整合能力強化

Unit 17 鷹眼：識破黑寡婦的真為人、鋼鐵人的啟發

Born in Waverly, Iowa, Clint Barton had a brother named Barney Barton. The borthers eventually joined the Carson Carnival of Traveling Wonders. One day, Clint accidentally **1.** _____ out that the Swordsman was **2.** _____ money from the carnival. Clint was **3.** _____ and tried to report to the owner. However, before he could do so, he was already beaten up by the Swordsman before he **4.** _____. Even so, Barney didn't have any **5.** _____ on Clint. Instead, Barney blamed Clint for not sharing the **6.** _____ and abandoned him since. Clint left the Carson Carnival and started to use his **7.** _____ archery skills to work in various carnivals as "Hawkeye". He was also known as "The World's Greatest Marksman." Once during his performance, he **8.** _____ Iron Man saving lives. He was so **9.** _____ and soon decided to become a **10.** _____ crime fighter.

However, at the first night on **11.** _____, he was mistaken for a criminal by police and was hunted down. He met the Black Widow, a **12.** _____ for the Soviet Union. She falsely led him to believe he could get the **13.** _____ from Iron man if he defeats him. Later on, he **14.** _____ who the Black Widow really is and how she was trying to **15.** _____ his thoughts. Hawkeye **16.** _____ his decision and hoped to join the Avengers.

A	regretted	**B**	fortune
C	wised up	**D**	manipulate
E	spy	**F**	terrified
G	found	**H**	sympathy
I	technology	**J**	natural
K	patrol	**L**	embezzling
M	inspired	**N**	costumed
O	escaped	**P**	witnessed

出生於愛荷華州為弗利，柯林‧巴頓有一個名為巴尼‧巴頓的哥哥。兄弟倆最終加入旅遊奇蹟的卡森移動樂園。有一天，柯林無意間發現劍客笑挪用樂園的資金。柯林嚇壞了，並試圖向業主報告。但是，他還沒來得及這樣做前，就已經被劍客毆打，劍客也逃跑了。即便如此，巴尼並沒有同情柯林。相反的，巴尼指責柯林沒有共享財富，因此拋棄了他。柯林離開了卡森移動樂園，並開始利用他與生俱來的射箭技能，以「鷹眼」的名號在不同的嘉年華工作。在他表演的期間，也被稱為是「世界上最偉大的射手」。有一次，他親眼目睹了鋼鐵人拯救生命。他因此精神振奮，很快就決定成為一個喬裝的打擊犯罪戰士。

然而，在巡邏的第一個晚上，他被警方誤認為罪犯而被追殺。在逃跑時，他遇到了蘇聯間諜黑寡婦。他很快地愛上了她。黑寡婦使他相信他希望可以打敗鋼鐵人，並從他那裡偷技術。後來，他識破了黑寡婦的真為人，也了解到她是如何試圖操縱他的想法。鷹眼後悔自己的決定，並希望加入復仇者。

▶▶ 參考答案

1. G	2. L
3. F	4. O
5. H	6. B
7. J	8. P
9. M	10. N
11. K	12. E
13. I	14. C
15. D	16. A

Part 1 同義字模擬試題

Part 2 填空題模擬試題

Part 3 聽、讀整合能力強化

Unit 18 鷹眼：沒有超能力的超級英雄

He broke into the Avengers Mansion and **1.** _____ his powers with the help from the butler, Edwin Jarvis. Iron Man saw how **2.** _____ Hawkeye was about becoming a hero. Therefore, he **3.** _____ for Hawkeye to be a member of the Avengers. He was once **4.** _____ involved with the Scarlet Witch and was met with **5.** _____ from her brother, Quicksilver. The **6.** _____ didn't last because Hawkeye was still in love with the Black Widow. Hawkeye once **7.** _____ Captain America's leadership before, but over time he came to **8.** _____ him and see him as a mentor.

Even though Hawkeye doesn't have superhuman powers, he is at the **9.** _____ of human conditions. Being trained in the **10.** _____ since he was a kid, he is also an **11.** _____ fencer, acrobat and marksman. Hawkeye uses a 250 pounds forced raw weight bow which no one else is capable of drawing the string to **12.** _____ an arrow Hawkeye was also **13.** _____ by Captain America in martial arts and hand-to-hand **14.** _____ so he has no problem fighting the villains without his weapons. He even has a **15.** _____ for being able to turn any **16.** _____ into a weapon.

A	combat	**B**	relationship
C	peak	**D**	serious
E	displayed	**F**	romantically
G	circus	**H**	hostility
I	trained	**J**	vouched
K	doubted	**L**	respect
M	reputation	**N**	launch
O	exceptional	**P**	object

他闖進了復仇者大廈，並在管家愛德恩・賈維斯的幫助下顯示他的能力。鋼鐵人看到鷹眼是多麼認真希望成為一位英雄。因此，他擔保了鷹眼成為復仇者的成員。鷹眼也曾與猩紅巫婆有著浪漫的關係，因此而和她哥哥快銀之間有了敵意。這段感情並沒有持續，因為鷹眼還是愛著黑寡婦。鷹眼曾經懷疑過美國隊長的領導，但隨著時間的推移，他變得尊重他，並視他為導師。

雖然鷹眼沒有超能力，但是他人類能力條件卻是處於最高峰。因為在孩童時期便在馬戲團裡接受訓練，他因此也是一個出色的擊劍運動員、雜技演員和射手。鷹眼採用的是 250 磅中的畫弓，沒有人能夠拉得動他的弓箭來發射箭頭。鷹眼也被美國隊長訓練武術和肉搏戰術，因此就算沒有武器，他可以與敵人對戰。他甚至有能夠把任何物體變為武器的聲譽。

▶▶ 參考答案

1. E	2. D
3. J	4. F
5. H	6. B
7. K	8. L
9. C	10. G
11. O	12. N
13. I	14. A
15. M	16. P

Unit 19 捷射：在陰影中成長、射殺兄長

Growing up with Hawkeye in the carnival, Barney has been living in the **1.** _____. Without a mentorlike the Swordsman, Barney was working as his brother's **2.** _____. He became jealous and **3.** _____ from Clint. One time, when Clint found out that Swordsman was embezzling **4.** _____ from the carnival, Barney **5.** _____ Clint for going against Swordsman. Barney got tired of the circus life and decided to join the US army. He did ask his brother to join him. Barney gave Clint an **6.** _____, to join him or lose his brother. Barney **7.** _____ his brother to show up, but Clint never did. Barney left **8.** _____.

Barney later on became an FBI Agent after his **9.** _____ in the Army. Most of the time, he worked **10.** _____. Once, he was working undercover as a **11.** _____ for a criminal named Marko. At that time, Clint already created his new **12.** _____ "Hawkeye" and was working with his new **13.** _____ from the carnival Trick Shot to rob Marko's **14.** _____. He **15.** _____ Barney and before Barney could **16.** _____ who he was, he left.

A	money	**B**	mansion
C	disappointedly	**D**	shadow
E	ultimatum	**F**	assistant
G	mentor	**H**	distant
I	stint	**J**	waited for
K	undercover	**L**	condemned
M	identity	**N**	bodyguard
O	shot	**P**	figure out

Part 1 同義字模擬試題

Part 2 填空題模擬試題

Part 3 聽、讀整合能力強化

在移動樂園中與鷹眼一起長大，巴尼一直生活在陰影之中。沒有一個像劍客一樣的良師益友，巴尼工作就是作為弟弟的助手。他嫉妒柯林並開始遠離柯林。有一次，當柯林發現劍士從移動樂園裡挪用資金，巴尼竟然譴責柯林特違背劍客。巴尼厭倦了馬戲團的生活，並決定加入美國軍隊。他要他的弟弟和他一起。巴尼給了柯林最後通牒，要他加入或失去他的兄弟。巴尼等著弟弟露面，但柯林並沒有。巴尼失望地離開。

巴尼他在退出軍隊後，後來成為 FBI 探員。大多數時候，他身為臥底。有一次，他臥底為一個名為馬爾科的罪犯的保鏢。當時，柯林已經創造了他的新身份「鷹眼」，並與他的新導師「捷射」一起搶劫馬爾科的豪宅。他槍殺哥哥巴尼，而在巴尼能分辨出他到底是誰時他離開了。

▶▶ 參考答案

1.	D	2.	F
3.	H	4.	A
5.	L	6.	E
7.	J	8.	C
9.	I	10.	K
11.	N	12.	M
13.	G	14.	B
15.	O	16.	P

Part 1 同義字模擬試題

Part 2 填空題模擬試題

Part 3 聽、讀整合能力強化

Barney turned down another cover mission, which made Egghead pissed off. Egghead **1.** _____ his FBI team. Barney went to the Avengers for help but ended up **2.** _____ himself, to stop Egghead's ray projector from **3.** _____ others. At his **4.** _____, Clint finally found out about his brother's double life, and the fact that his brother was fully **5.** _____ of Clint's double life as well.

Barney's body was kept in as tasis by Egghead. Years later Zemo **6.** _____ Barney's background and **7.** _____ him and manipulated him to go against Hawkeye. Zemo then found Hawkeye's other mentor, Trick Shot. Trick Shot was suffering from **8.** _____. Zemo promised to fund Trick Shot's **9.** _____ treatment if he taught Barney how to **10.** _____ a bow. Trick Shot did so, but did not **11.** _____ the fund he was promised. Before Trick Shot dies, Zemo dropped Trick Shot off to Hawkeye and left a **12.** _____ with a bow. When Clint was investigating his mentor's death, Barney **13.** _____ him and declared himself as the NEW TRICK SHOT. He **14.** _____ Clint to Zemo. Zemo then arranged the brothers to fight to the death. Hawkeye was able to defeat Barney and capture him alive. The relationship between the brothers did not **15.** _____ though. As the NEW TRICK SHOT, Barney was later on invited to become the **16.** _____ of the Dark Avengers to replace Bullseye as the new Dark Hawkeye.

A	recover	**B**	message
C	destroyed	**D**	revived
E	medical	**F**	sacrificing
G	receive	**H**	cancer
I	wield	**J**	aware
K	ambushed	**L**	funeral
M	incarnation	**N**	harming
O	dug up	**P**	captured

巴尼拒絕另一個臥底任務，因而惹怒了理論家。理論家毀了他的
FBI團隊。巴尼跑到復仇者那裡尋求幫助，但最後還是犧牲了自己，以
防止理論家的射線投影傷害到其他人。在他的葬禮時，柯林終於知道
了他哥哥的雙重生活，而事實上，他的哥哥也完全知道柯林的雙重生
活。

理論家讓巴尼的血流停滯。幾年後澤莫挖出了巴尼的背景，使他
甦醒過來，並操縱他與鷹眼作對。澤莫隨後發現鷹眼的其他導師，捷
射。捷射身患癌症。澤莫答應資助捷射的治療，條件是如果他教巴尼
如何使用弓。捷射這樣做了，但沒有收到他承諾的資金。捷射在死之
前，澤莫將他丟給鷹眼，並留了一只弓當作留言。當柯林正在調查他
的恩師之死時，巴尼伏擊他並宣布自己為新的捷射。他捕捉到柯林並
將他交給澤莫。澤莫之後安排兄弟決一死戰。鷹眼擊敗了巴尼並活捉
了他。兄弟之間的關係，終究沒有恢復。作為新的捷射，巴尼後來就
受邀成為黑暗復仇者的化身，以取代「靶眼」作為新的闇黑鷹眼。

▶▶ 參考答案

1. C	2. F
3. N	4. L
5. J	6. O
7. D	8. H
9. E	10. I
11. G	12. B
13. K	14. P
15. A	16. M

Unit 21 黑寡婦：黑寡婦計劃、蛇蠍美人

Natasha Romanova was an orphan who was **1.** _____ in a burning building during an attack on Stalingrad by enemy forces. She was found and **2.** _____ by a Soviet soldier named Petrovitch Bezukhov, who later on became her dearest friend and father figure. In 1941, she was almost **3.** _____ by the ninja clan "the Hand", but was **4.** _____ saved by Logan. She then was recruited to become part of the Black Widow Program which was a team of **5.** _____ female agents. At the program, all female agents were biotechnologically and psycho-technologically **6.** _____. They all have unusual young look like they never aged, they are also **7.** _____ to diseases and heal at an above human rate. They were all **8.** _____ with false memories to ensure their **9.** _____.

Natasha was trained to become a world class **10.** _____, acrobat, and aerialist capable of numerous **11.** _____ and feats. Since she was **12.** _____ to be a ballerina, she also learned **13.** _____ ballet skill as well. During her training days, she fell shortly in love with her **14.** _____ Winter Soldier. However, she was later on **15.** _____ to marry a champion test pilot, Alexi Shostakov. Natasha did end up falling in love with Shostakov, but the KGB **16.** _____ Shostakov's death and made Natasha a real widow. Natasha was described as a femme fatale.

A	instructor	**B**	elite
C	resistant	**D**	enhanced
E	characterized	**F**	rescued
G	athlete	**H**	trapped
I	deployed	**J**	maneuvers
K	luckily	**L**	brainwashed
M	loyalty	**N**	faked
O	arranged	**P**	marvelous

Part 1 同義字模擬試題

Part 2 填空題模擬試題

Part 3 聽、讀整合能力強化

▶▶▶ 中譯

　　娜塔莎諾娃是個在被敵軍斯大林格勒的一次襲擊中，被困在正在燃燒中大樓的孤兒。她是被一位名為彼得羅維奇的蘇聯士兵所發現的。這個人後來成為了她最親密的朋友和父親。1941 年，她幾乎被忍者家族的「合手黨」給洗腦了，但幸運的被洛根所救。然後，她被招募進入黑寡婦計劃，一個精英女特工團隊。在訓練中，所有的女特工的生物技術和心理技術皆被增強。她們都具有異於常人的年輕樣貌及年齡不會增長的技能。她們也可以抵抗疾病，並可以以快於人類的速度癒合。他們都用虛假記憶部署，以確保她們的忠誠度。

　　娜塔莎被培養成為一名世界級的運動員、雜技演員和一個可以進行各種演習和功勳的高空達人。因為她的特點是一個芭蕾舞演員，她也學會了了不起的芭蕾舞技巧。在她接受訓練時，她便愛上了她的教練寒天戰士。不過，她後來被安排嫁給一個冠軍的試飛員，阿列克謝。娜塔莎最終是愛上了阿列克謝，但 KGB 偽造了阿列克謝的死，使得娜塔莎成為一位真正的寡婦。娜塔莎被描述為一個蛇蠍美人。

▶▶ 參考答案

1.	H	2.	F
3.	L	4.	K
5.	B	6.	D
7.	C	8.	I
9.	M	10.	G
11.	J	12.	E
13.	P	14.	A
15.	O	16.	N

Part 1 同義字模擬試題

Part 2 填空題模擬試題

Part 3 聽、讀整合能力強化

Her first mission was to assist Boris Turgenov in the **1.** _____ of Professor Anton Vanko for **2.** _____ from the Soviet Union. They **3.** _____ Stark Industries and manipulated **4.** _____ from American defense contractor Tony Strak. Fortunately, Iron Man showed up and inevitably **5.** _____ Natasha. Iron Man and the two went into battle. Vanko **6.** _____ himself to save Iron Man and killed Turgenov at the same time. Later on, Natasha met Hawkeye and **7.** _____ him to go against Iron Man. However, during a fight in between Hawkeye and Iron Man, Black Widow was badly injured. In order to save her, Hawkeye **8.** _____ to get her to safety. Falling in love with Hawkeye, Natasha's loyalty to her country was **9.** _____. Even so, she still left Hawkeye. She once again was **10.** _____ and battled the Avengers. Although, she eventually **11.** _____ the help from Hawkeye, she broke free from her **12.** _____ condition.

Later on, she joined the S.H.I.E.L.D. and started the **13.** _____ missions. She was then romantically **14.** _____ with Matt Murdock who later on became the Daredevil in San Francisco. They operated as **15.** _____ superheroes. After they broke up, Natasha then **16.** _____ to Los Angeles and formed a new super team known as The Champions, but group didn't last long.

A	brainwashed	**B**	assassination
C	manipulated	**D**	independent
E	information	**F**	defecting
G	retreated	**H**	international
I	sacrificed	**J**	infiltrated
K	weakened	**L**	confronted
M	psychological	**N**	moved
O	involved	**P**	received

Part 1 同義字模擬試題

Part 2 填空題模擬試題

Part 3 聽、讀整合能力強化

▶▶ 中譯

　　她的第一個任務是幫助包里斯刺殺從蘇聯叛逃的安東萬科教授。他們滲透進史塔克產業，並操縱美國國防承包商托尼史塔克的信息。還好，鋼鐵人出現了，無可避免地面對娜塔莎。鋼鐵人與他們兩位開始互戰。萬科犧牲自己來拯救鋼鐵人，並在同一時間殺死了包里斯後來，娜塔莎遇到鷹眼並開始操縱他，使他與鋼鐵人作對。然而，在鷹眼和鋼鐵人之間的戰鬥中，黑寡婦受了重傷。為了她的安全，鷹眼撤退，並帶她到安全的地方。在她愛上鷹眼的同時，娜塔莎對她國家的忠誠度也逐漸減弱。即便如此，她還是離開了鷹眼。她再次被洗腦並且與復仇者作戰。雖然她最終得到來自鷹眼的幫助，突破了她的心理狀態。後來，她加入了 S.H.I.E.L.D. 並啟動了國際任務。

　　然後，她與之後變身為夜行俠的馬特默多克在一起。他們住在舊金山。並作為獨立的超級英雄。他們分手後，娜塔莎則搬到了洛杉磯，並組成了一個「成功者」的球隊。但這個集團並沒有持續多久。

▶▶ 參考答案

1.	B	2.	F
3.	J	4.	E
5.	L	6.	I
7.	C	8.	G
9.	K	10.	A
11.	P	12.	M
13.	H	14.	O
15.	D	16.	N

Part 1 同義字模擬試題

Part 2 填空題模擬試題

Part 3 聽、讀整合能力強化

Unit 23 紅衛士：技術高超的運動員

Born in Moscow, Alexei Shastakov was known for being the Black Widow Natasha Romanova's **1.** _____. Both of them were agents of the Soviets. During World War II, Alexei shot down a large number of Luftwaffe fighter planes in **2.** _____ battles and was **3.** _____ for helping the Soviet Air Force win air **4.** _____ over the skies of Stalingrad and Kursk. Alexei was considered one of the most **5.** _____ pilots of the Soviet Union. He was also the first **6.** _____ who test flew the Mig 15. Later on, he fought against the U.S Air Force during the Korean War. He was then **7.** _____ to marry the famous ballerina, Natasha Romanova.

As the Cold War **8.** _____ up, the Soviet government realized that the country needed an **9.** _____ to Captain America. Alexi became the chosen one. During a mission away from home, Alexi was **10.** _____ of the new plans and was told not to have any **11.** _____ with any of his past friends and **12.** _____. He was not allowed to contact his wife either. Meanwhile, Natasha was informed by a Soviet **13.** _____ that Alexi had been killed in an **14.** _____ of an experimental rocket. The KGB **15.** _____ his death and started to train him in secrecy. He became a highly skilled athlete and was also **16.** _____ good at hand to hand combat.

A	faked	**B**	explosion
C	assigned	**D**	informed
E	flared	**F**	supremacy
G	typically	**H**	pilot
I	husband	**J**	acclaimed
K	official	**L**	contact
M	equivalent	**N**	aerial
O	credited	**P**	acquaintances

▶▶ 中譯

出生於莫斯科，阿列克謝是黑寡婦娜塔莎諾娃的丈夫。他們兩個都是蘇聯的特勤。二戰期間，阿列克謝擊落了大量的空軍戰機，並幫助蘇聯空軍贏得控制斯大林格勒和庫爾斯克天空的權利。阿列克謝可以說是蘇聯最知名的飛行員之一。他還在朝鮮戰爭期間進行米格 15 的測試。後來，他在韓戰期間與美軍對戰，爾後，被任命與著名的芭蕾舞演員娜塔莎羅曼諾娃結婚。

隨著冷戰爆發後，蘇聯政府意識到該國需要一個相當於美國隊長的人。阿列克謝成了不二人選。在一次離家的任務之中，阿列克謝得知這一新的計劃。他同時被告知不要跟任何過去的朋友和熟人做任何接觸。他也不能聯繫他的妻子。同時，娜塔莎也被蘇聯政府通知說阿列克謝已經在實驗火箭爆炸時被殺害。KGB 偽造了他的死亡，並開始他的秘密訓練。他成了一名技術高超的運動員，也善於肉搏戰。

▶▶ 參考答案

1. I	2. N
3. O	4. F
5. J	6. H
7. C	8. E
9. M	10. D
11. L	12. P
13. K	14. B
15. A	16. G

Unit 24 紅衛士：遇見黑寡婦、淹沒在熔岩底下

The KGB even made him his **1.** _____ weapon, the disc. The disc had a yellow hammer and **2.** _____ symbol on it to represent the Soviet Union. It is often times attached to his belt and can **3.** _____ return after being thrown using **4.** _____ forces. He also started to wear his new **5.** _____, and changed his name to the "Red Guardian."

Unlike the Black Widow who became **6.** _____ with the KGB, the Red Guardian remains **7.** _____ to his government. He even became more ruthless and **8.** _____. One time, he was sent to China to help protect a Communist Chinese **9.** _____ weapon located at a secret military **10.** _____ at an unknown location. He ended up **11.** _____ the Black Widow and Captain America. The Black Widow **12.** _____ something was familiar but couldn't tell what until the Red Guardian revealed his **13.** _____ identity to her. He was then shot and mortally **14.** _____. He then was buried under molten lava. Years later, he was revealed to be **15.** _____ and had risen very high in power within Bulgaria and Ronin. He started his mission to catch his former wife and **16.** _____ her for the crimes.

A	base	**B**	noticed
C	automatically	**D**	signature
E	vindictive	**F**	secret
G	costume	**H**	sickle
I	encountering	**J**	disillusioned
K	loyal	**L**	magnetic
M	true	**N**	wounded
O	try	**P**	alive

Part 1 同義字模擬試題

Part 2 填空題模擬試題

Part 3 聽、讀整合能力強化

▶▶ 中譯

KGB 甚至給了他知名武器，光盤。光盤上有一個黃色錘子和鐮刀的象徵，代表了蘇聯。它往往把光盤放在腰帶上，且可以使用磁力讓被拋出後的光盤自動返回。他也開始穿他的新服裝，並改名為「紅衛士」。

不像黑寡婦對 KGB 幻滅，紅衛士仍然忠於他的政府。他甚至變得更加無情和鬥氣。有一次，他被派往中國，以幫助保護中國共產黨一個位於秘密軍事基地處於未揭露位置的神秘武器。最後他遇到了黑寡婦和美國隊長。黑寡婦覺得很熟悉卻說不出什麼，直到紅衛士暴露了他的真實身份讓她知道。然後，他中槍，受了致命傷。爾後淹沒在熔岩底下。多年以後，有人透露他還活著，並活躍在保加利亞和羅寧。他的能力有著大大的進步。他開始了他的使命追捕他的前妻，並審判她的罪行。

▶▶ 參考答案

1.	D	2.	H
3.	C	4.	L
5.	G	6.	J
7.	K	8.	E
9.	F	10.	A
11.	I	12.	B
13.	M	14.	N
15.	P	16.	O

Part 1 同義字模擬試題

Part 2 填空題模擬試題

Part 3 聽、讀整合能力強化

Unit 25 浩克：童年的悲劇所造成的人格分裂、無限的力量

It's hard for most people to imagine being born in a family with **1. _____** parents. Unfortunately, Robert Bruce Banner was one of those kids. The son of an **2. _____**, Banner was hated by his atomic **3. _____** father who worked on producing clean **4. _____** power as an energy source. Dr. Brian Banner believed that his son's intelligence came from the **5. _____** to the nuclear power. He believed that his son had been mutated and was indeed a **6. _____**. Banner's mother tried to stop Brian but ended up getting **7. _____**. Brian was then sent to a **8. _____** institute. Due to the childhood **9. _____**, Banner developed a **10. _____** personality. He found it hard to develop **11. _____** and often being picked on while he was in school. One day, he built and planted a **12. _____** in his school which caused the explosion. Of course, he was not only expelled but also caught the military's **13. _____**. Banner was later hired by the military after he earned a **14. _____** in nuclear physics.

An ignorant teenager wandered onto the testing field, while he was supervising the trial of an experimental gamma bomb he designed. To save him, Bruce was struck by bomb blast, causing some strange transformation in his body. At first, he will transform into a brutish gray Hulk only at sunset and **15. _____** to human form at dawn. Then, he would change into the childlike green Hulk when he gets intensely excited. Since the transformation, the Hulk also gained the **16. _____** strength. He was able to take Superman and Thor with his hands tied behind his back.

A	bomb	**B**	psychiatric
C	nuclear	**D**	abusive
E	exposure	**F**	murdered
G	friendships	**H**	alcoholic
I	revert	**J**	monster
K	split	**L**	physicist
M	doctorate	**N**	attention
O	unlimited	**P**	tragedy

▶▶ 中譯

　　大多數人都難以想像出生在有會虐待孩子的父母的家庭。不幸的是，羅伯特・布魯斯・班寧就是那些孩子之一。一個酒鬼的兒子，班寧被父親所憎恨，他父親是個酒鬼，也是一位核能原子物理學家，致力生產環保核能。布萊恩・班寧博士相信他兒子的聰穎是從曝光到核電所得到的。他認為，他的兒子已經突變並確實是一個怪物。班寧的母親試圖阻止布萊恩，但最終被殺害。然後布萊恩就被送往精神病研究所。由於童年的悲劇，班寧產生了人格分裂。他發現他很難發展友誼，他在學校時，經常被欺負。有一天他在學校製作並埋了一個炸彈，引發爆炸。他當然被開除了，但同時也引起了軍方的重視。班寧後來在獲得核物理學博士後，被軍方聘請。

　　正當他在指揮一個他設計的伽瑪炸彈的實驗時，一個無知的少年遊蕩到測試領域。為了救他，布魯斯被炸彈所擊中，導致了身體有了奇怪的轉變。起初，他會變成一個粗野的灰色巨人，只在日落食變身，在黎明時恢復人形。然後，當他強烈興奮時，他會改變成綠色，像孩子的浩克。自轉型以來，浩克也獲得了無限的力量。即使他的雙手被反綁在背後，他還是能夠擊敗超人和雷神。

▶▶ 參考答案

1.	D	2.	H
3.	L	4.	C
5.	E	6.	J
7.	F	8.	B
9.	P	10.	K
11.	G	12.	A
13.	N	14.	M
15.	I	16.	O

Part 1 同義字模擬試題

Part 2 填空題模擬試題

Part 3 聽、讀整合能力強化

Unit 26 浩克：浩克的誕生、總統的特赦

He can also create a large thunderclap-type **1.** _____ force to hurt enemies, to put out fire or **2.** _____ people. His legs are **3.** _____ so much that he can travel miles in a single jump. His skin allows protection from bullets, **4.** _____, and rockets. He also has the quickest healing factor and the ability to **5.** _____ mind control.

Since his transformation, he was **6.** _____ by the military forces continually, but later he helped the government to **7.** _____ the alien Metal Master and received a presidential **8.** _____. After that, he teamed up with many superheroes who thought he wasn't all bad. Starting from Spider-Man and Iron Fist to the Avengers like the Thing and Wolverine, they all partnered with Hulk on several **9.** _____. They fought against him too since the Hulk has the split **10.** _____ which he couldn't control easily. Because of the **11.** _____, the Hulk could easily be **12.** _____ and used by the villains in short time to harm people too. Gamma-powered **13.** _____ Leonard "Doc" Samson once captured the Hulk and successfully **14.** _____ Banner and the Hulk. This action made the Hulk the ultimate monster who only has the **15.** _____ but doesn't have the intelligence to control his actions. Realizing the only solution to rein in the Hulk is to **16.** _____ with the monster again, Banner did so.

A	separated	**B**	occasions
C	personality	**D**	resist
E	pardon	**F**	psychiatrist
G	disadvantage	**H**	augmented
I	strength	**J**	destroy
K	manipulated	**L**	deafen
M	hunted	**N**	merge
O	concussive	**P**	grenades

Part 1 同義字模擬試題

Part 2 填空題模擬試題

Part 3 聽、讀整合能力強化

▶▶ 中譯

　　他也可以創建一個大霹靂式的震盪來傷害敵人，滅火或使人變聾。他的腿力大增，一個跳躍即可行走好幾英里。他的皮膚可以防子彈、手榴彈和火箭。他還擁有最快的癒合因子和不被精神控制的能力。

　　由於他的轉變，他不斷地被軍隊捕殺，直到後來，他幫助政府消滅外星金屬隊長，並獲得總統特赦。之後，他與許多認為他也不完全是壞人的超級英雄們聯手。從蜘蛛人開始，到鐵拳、復仇者的金剛狼和石頭人等，他們都與浩克合作多次。他們與他也對立過，因為浩克有分裂的人格，他不能輕易控制。因為這個缺點，浩克很容易被操縱，並被壞人短時間的利用來傷害人類。伽瑪力學的心理醫生倫納德「醫師」山森有一次捕獲浩克，並成功的分離了班寧和浩克。這個舉動使得浩克成為了一個只有蠻力但沒有足夠的智慧來控制自己行動的怪物。了解到惟有再與浩克結合才能解決這個問題，班寧就這麼做了。

▶▶ 參考答案

1. O		2. L	
3. H		4. P	
5. D		6. M	
7. J		8. E	
9. B		10. C	
11. G		12. K	
13. F		14. A	
15. I		16. N	

Part 1 同義字模擬試題

Part 2 填空題模擬試題

Part 3 聽、讀整合能力強化

Unit 27　首腦：暴露於伽瑪射線、總統的特赦

Samuel Sterns had a not so happy **1.** _____. He eventually dropped out of high school. One day, when Samuel was moving a **2.** _____ of radioactive waste, he was caught in an **3.** _____ explosion. Just like the Hulk, he was exposed to the Gamma **4.** _____. He was soon sent to the ER, but while he was **5.** _____ in the hospital, he started to have an **6.** _____ thirst for knowledge. He started to read through everything he could lay his hands on. Weeks later, his **7.** _____ turned green and his skull **8.** _____ upwards. He transformed into the hyper-intelligent Leader. His intelligence allows him to **9.** _____ possibilities and the outcomes are **10.** _____ correct. His assumptions are almost correct and he is able to **11.** _____ any events because of his perfect **12.** _____. He also has the ability to control other people's minds. Because of his **13.** _____ childhood, he decided to use intelligence to bring him the power and the **14.** _____ life which he didn't have before.

He then organized a spy ring to steal **15.** _____ secrets. He became the most consistent and dangerous creature who **16.** _____ to take over the United States and eventually conquer the world.

A	scientific	**B**	expanded
C	memory	**D**	cylinder
E	childhood	**F**	skin
G	unexpected	**H**	prestigious
I	recovering	**J**	insatiable
K	normally	**L**	radiation
M	predict	**N**	desires
O	recall	**P**	miserable

▶▶▶ 中譯

塞繆·史塔恩有著不那麼幸福的童年。他最終在高中輟學。有一天，當塞繆在移動放射性廢物缸時，他陷入了一個意想不到的爆炸。就像浩克，他接觸到伽瑪輻射。他很快被送到急診室，但是當他在醫院恢復時，他開始對知識有著貪得無厭的渴求。他開始閱讀一切他拿得到的東西。幾個星期後，他的皮膚變成綠色，他的頭骨向上擴展。他變成永存於人們心中的英雄霸主超級智能領導者。他的智慧讓他能預測可能性，而且結果通常是正確的。他的假設也通常是正確的，他能夠完美的記憶任何事件。他也有能力控制別人的心靈。由於他苦難的童年，他決定用智慧，帶給他力量和他以前沒有信譽的生活。

爾後，他組織了一個間諜網，專偷科學秘密。他成為了最一貫的和危險的生物，夢想要接手美國並最終統治世界。

▶▶ 參考答案

1.	E	2.	D
3.	G	4.	L
5.	I	6.	J
7.	F	8.	B
9.	M	10.	K
11.	O	12.	C
13.	P	14.	H
15.	A	16.	N

Unit 28 首腦：統治世界的夢想、重拾力量

Both transformed by the Gamma radiation, the Leader first thought that the Hulk would join his spy **1.** _____ without a doubt. However, things went differently. The Hulk became an **2.** _____ to his plan. Instead of fighting against the superhero teams, the Hulk actually group up with them to **3.** _____ with the Leader. Desperate to study his foe, the Leader first sent the Chameleon and **4.** _____ humanoids to capture the Hulk.

This action stated the non-stop **5.** _____ between the two of them. The desire to conquer the world led the Leader to **6.** _____ an army of powerful **7.** _____ plastic robots called Humanoids and a space station named Omnivac. He also recruited a whole bunch of **8.** _____ such as Rhino, Abomination and Half-Life. He sometimes partnered with General "Thunderbolt" Ross and MODOK.

One day, the Leader's mutation **9.** _____, and he reverted back to the ordinary Samuel Sterns. In order to regain his **10.** _____ intellect, he drained gamma radiation from Rick Jones who was also suffering from the gamma radiation **11.** _____. The Leader gained his power back. He later on created an **12.** _____ community hidden beneath the Columbia ice-fields of Alberta, Canada and named it Freehold. It was a place filled with people who are dying from radiation **13.** _____. The Leader told the people there that Freehold would become the new **14.** _____.

However, in reality, he was using the radiation victims for **15.** _____. The Leader was once killed in a battle with the Hulk; however, his mind survived. His mind had **16.** _____ beyond the need for a body.

A	isolated	**B**	ring
C	destabilized	**D**	synthetic
E	combat	**F**	construct
G	obedient	**H**	impediment
I	poisoning	**J**	villains
K	heightened	**L**	feud
M	evolved	**N**	experiments
O	transformation	**P**	society

由於兩個都是被伽瑪射線所改變，首腦毫無疑問的原本想要叫浩克加入他的間諜網。然而，事情進展並不相同。浩克成為了阻礙他計劃的人。與其與超級英雄們對戰，浩克與他們團結一同對抗首腦。渴望了解他的敵人，首腦首先送了變色龍和合成人去捕捉浩克。

這個動作開始了他們兩個人之間不停的爭執。想要統治世界的慾望導致首腦來構建強大的塑料機器人，被稱為類人生物的軍隊和一個名為 Omnivac 的航空站。他還找來一大堆壞人，如犀牛，憎惡和半條命。他有時也會與大將軍「迅雷」羅斯和 MODOK 合作。

有一天，首腦的突變動搖了，他恢復到普通的塞繆·史塔恩。為了奪回自己的高智力，他喝乾了也為改造而痛苦的瑞克·瓊斯身上的伽瑪射線。首腦重新獲得了他的力量。他後來在加拿大阿爾伯塔省的哥倫比亞冰下創造了一個孤立的社區，稱為永久業權。這個地方充滿了因為輻射中毒而快要死亡的人類。首腦告訴那裡的人說，永久業權將成為新的社會。

然而，在現實中，他使用了輻射受害者進行實驗。首腦在與浩克的一場戰鬥時一度被殺害。然而，他的腦活了下來。後來他的腦已經演變成不需要身體也可以運作。

▶▶ 參考答案

1.	B	2.	H
3.	E	4.	D
5.	L	6.	F
7.	G	8.	J
9.	C	10.	K
11.	O	12.	A
13.	I	14.	P
15.	N	16.	M

附錄 Part 2 答案表

Unit 1

1.	KQ	2.	AFS	3.	VR	4.	WE	5	M	6.	XO
7.	BT	8.	N	9.	AFS	10.	GC	11.	PH	12.	IJ

Unit 2

13.	D	14.	ET	15.	NR	16.	GO	17.	X	18.	MV
19.	Q	20.	FL	21.	IU	22.	AS	23.	P	24.	B

Unit 3

25.	AK	26.	BF	27.	GL	28.	MQ	29.	H	30.	E
31.	NX	32.	CW	33.	V	34.	JO	35.	RU	36.	PS

Unit 4

37.	DP	38.	HQ	39.	NU	40.	A	41.	BR	42.	CL
43.	G	44.	E	45.	FT	46.	IX	47.	M	48.	V

Unit 5

49.	W	50.	EL	51.	GS	52.	HN	53.	T	54.	CO
55.	B	56.	KM	57.	DF	58.	UX	59.	IR	60.	V

Unit 6

61.	BE	62.	HK	63.	G	64.	RX	65.	AP	66.	V
67.	CF	68.	QT	69.	DI	70.	JO	71.	MU	72.	L

Unit 7

73.	AX	74.	KQ	75.	GP	76.	W	77.	BV	78.	JO
79.	CL	80.	FR	81.	S	82.	IU	83.	H	84.	M

Unit 8

85. E	86. GM	87. H	88. FO	89. QR	90. N
91. BJ	92. P	93. T	94. DW	95. I	96. S

Unit 9

97. G	98. EW	99. T	100. NQ	101. AK	102. V
103. JM	104. OX	105. DH	106. I	107. B	108. FR

Unit 10

109. Q	110. BC	111. OX	112. I	113. H	114. NT
115. A	116. D	117. R	118. G	119. V	120. PS

Unit 11

121. JV	122. BE	123. S	124. W	125. QX	126. CG
127. NU	128. K	129. DF	130. IM	131. H	132. A

Unit 12

133. DJ	134. HN	135. QT	136. CU	137. LR	138. KP
139. IO	140. GM	141. AW	142. B	143. S	144. F

Unit 13

145. EK	146. D	147. LO	148. I	149. A	150. CV
151. TW	152. MP	153. G	154. S	155. J	156. N

Unit 14

157. EHN	158. EHN	159. TU	160. FO	161. CR	162. VX
163. L	164. A	165. D	166. G	167. Q	168. M

國家圖書館出版品預行編目(CIP)資料

雅思單字聖經：模擬試題/Amanda Chou著.
-- 初版. -- 新北市：倍斯特出版事業有限公司
, 2023.03面；公分. -- (考用英語系列；042)
ISBN 978-626-96563-3-2(平裝)
1.CST: 國際英語語文測試系統 2.CST: 詞彙

805.189   111020963

考用英語系列 042

雅思單字聖經-模擬試題（英式發音附QR code音檔）

初　　刷　　2023年3月
定　　價　　新台幣499元

作　　者　　Amanda Chou
出　　版　　倍斯特出版事業有限公司
發 行 人　　周瑞德
電　　話　　886-2-8245-6905
傳　　真　　886-2-2245-6398
地　　址　　23558 新北市中和區立業路83巷7號4樓
E - m a i l　　best.books.service@gmail.com
官　　網　　www.bestbookstw.com
總 編 輯　　齊心瑀
企劃編輯　　陳韋佑
封面構成　　高鍾琪
內頁構成　　菩薩蠻數位文化有限公司
印　　製　　大亞彩色印刷製版股份有限公司

港澳地區總經銷　　泛華發行代理有限公司
地　　址　　香港新界將軍澳工業邨駿昌街7號2樓
電　　話　　852-2798-2323
傳　　真　　852-3181-3973